Her Billionaire Cowboy Fake Fiancé

She's a free spirit worth billions and he's just a small town sheriff. They've been dancing around each other for years but now she needs a favor...

Caroline McCoy is not happy with her grandfather and his quest for marrying off her and her brothers. She's especially not happy that he's decided that Sheriff Jesse James is the right man for her. Sparks are about to fly and everyone better take cover!

Two Billionaire Brothers determined to marry off their grandsons...one is going to do it even from the grave using his last will and testament...can the other do it before it's too late!

HER BILLIONAIRE COWBOY FAKE FIANCÉ

McCoy Billionaire Brothers, Book Six

HOPE
MOORE

Her Billionaire Cowboy Fake Fiancé
Copyright © 2020 Hope Moore

HER BILLIONAIRE COWBOY FAKE FIANCÉ

McCoy Billionaire Brothers, Book Six

HOPE MOORE

Her Billionaire Cowboy Fake Fiancé
Copyright © 2020 Hope Moore

CHAPTER ONE

The dance benefiting the boys home near Stonewall was a good Texas tradition in small towns across the state. Joy and excitement filled Caroline McCoy at the sight of all the people who had come out in force to support this wonderful cause that was dear to her heart.

The music pounded out loud and proud around her. She loved, loved, *loved* street dances.

Loved them even more when they were for a good cause such as the boys ranch on the outskirts of town.

What she didn't like…was dancing with Sheriff Jesse James.

She would rather be dancing with a bear, but as he held her close and they two-stepped across the pavement among the happy crowd, she inhaled his fresh fragrance. He smelled of spicy aftershave, nothing expensive yet potent and dangerous on him, and it had her fighting the urge to bury her nose against his neck and breathe deeply. She shivered with an awareness that she did not want to feel. His hand spread wider on her lower back, easing her closer so that they moved as one. Heat swept through her like a blast of hot air on a windy day.

She met his dark gaze. "Stop holding me so close. The whole town is watching."

"What's new, heiress? They're going to gossip about us one way or the other." He tugged her a fraction closer.

He was enjoying this too much. He knew exactly what he was doing to her and though she fought it, her pulse charged forward like a runner out of the starting blocks. She tried to shut it down—it wasn't as though she hadn't danced with him before. But this last year, their push-pull relationship had escalated, and being this close to him was just no good for her.

She told her insides to get a grip and ignored how those chocolate eyes melted her knees and her insides again. But they ignored her.

"How's your girlfriend?" she asked, needling him. Really it was to remind herself that this cowboy flirted like crazy with her but that was all it would ever be between them. He had interest elsewhere, and most recently she'd seen him in Fredericksburg, shopping for little girl's clothes and then on the sidewalk with someone she didn't recognize. No, Jesse had no scarcity of girlfriends. The lawman was good-looking, self-assured, and drew women like flies. One more reason it irritated her that if she let down her guard, she could be one of them. She did not like being a lemming.

He dipped his chin and grinned. "You jealous, heiress?"

"Ha, I wouldn't be jealous of anybody with you."

He laughed and tugged her closer until she was pressed against him. "I don't believe you And to answer your question, I don't have a girlfriend. It didn't work out."

Heart rejoiced at the news that the woman she'd seen him with in Fredericksburg not long ago was not his girlfriend. Electricity hummed through her as the memory of them walking arm in arm down the steet nagged her. "You two sure looked cozy."

"I didn't say we weren't friends. We just agreed that was how we worked best so no need to be jealous."

"Not jealous." She stepped on his instep on purpose.

He grimaced but it quickly turned to a grin. "Now

that's jealousy."

Butterflies erupted in her lower stomach. *Dag gum their wings.* "Why do you insist on thinking I am in the least bit attracted to you, Sheriff?" "Because it's true. Look, I can't help it, either. I'm attracted to you, too. Doesn't mean I'm going to do anything about it except enjoy a dance with you. And give the good people of Stonewall something to talk about."

He spun them in a dizzy circle and then dipped her. He gave her a wink as she looked up at him from the horizontal position that she found herself in.

The man was incorrigible. She laughed, fighting the butterflies. "Oh, they are, no doubt about that. Now, are we going to dance and irritate each other, or are we going to discuss business?"

He pulled her back to standing position, his large hand still spread out on her lower back, and she was aware of every imprint of every finger as it burned a brand all the way through her.

Drat his very touch.

"Well, heiress. Here's the deal—the home is in trouble, I'm just not sure what's going on."

"What do they need? You know I'll get it or raise it."

"I know. They couldn't have survived this long

without the input of cash you keep pumping into it. They've talked about retiring for the last two years, but I have a feeling the talk is over and it's about to happen. They're getting older and that's not an easy job, wrangling all those boys. It's time to let somebody else take over. They've loved on many of us boys going through that place. Now it's time for them to relax a little bit. It's not like they don't have a whole herd of boys who love them dearly and want to see the best for them. But they can't keep up like they used to, so I'm encouraging them to turn it over to someone new."

Everything he said was true. But this was one of the reasons she found herself attracted to the irritating man. He might be cocky, he might be good at his job, but he had a heart as big as Texas. He had been raised on that boys ranch when he had been abandoned as a kid and loved Gladys and Mike dearly.

"I agree with you on all points." She saw concern in his eyes and her heart ached, knowing he was worried about them. "They're in their eighties, aren't they? Giving up their life's work will be hard for them."

"Yes, it will." He sighed and she saw a rare moment when his guard was down, giving her a glimpse at his concern.

"How many do you think they've taken in through the years?"

"I'm thinking in forty years with the place taking on six to eight guys at a time, it's nearly a hundred who have called the place home. And all the years I was there, it was full, you know that. Some came in older and others came in young like me and stayed until we grew out of the system."

They were moving slowly, oblivious of the music and the people around them as they were lost in their conversation. This was important and both had dropped their tug-of-war of attraction that they battled, because this was bigger than both of them.

"Who is going to take on the responsibility of it now?" She felt his hand slide up her back and her stomach tilted, reminding her that they were still locked in a two-step embrace.

His gaze dug deep into hers. "My time as a law enforcement officer is coming up for re-election and I'm thinking of not running so I can take over for them. I've got a couple of deputies, you know, who could easily run for my office and do well for the county."

Shock radiated through her. "Jesse, you're a law enforcement officer through and through. Are you sure you can do that?"

"Yeah, if I had a good enough reason. And there's only one other reason that I could think of that would ever get me to step down."

Her heart pounded as his gaze bore into hers. "And what is that other reason?" It was a dangerous question for her.

"If I ever found a woman I wanted to marry, who didn't want me in law enforcement, then that would be a good reason to step down and find something else. I've been saving up, you know, for my own ranch."

The thought of him marrying someone always caused her heart to ache in ways that nothing else could ever make it hurt. She liked that he would put his marriage first, his wife first over his career. She shoved the thought out of her head. "Well, I think that's very commendable of you. Now you'll just have to find a wife, I guess, who wants to be the mother of a herd of boys ranging from all ages."

His eyes narrowed and she didn't know whether he knew it, but they looked kind of sultry, really enticing, and maddingly heart-stopping. She misstepped and stomped his foot accidentally.

"Sorry. Didn't mean to stomp your foot with my high-heeled boot."

He grimaced slightly. "No problem. Thankfully my rawhide boots are thick."

"That is a good thing. So I guess if I accidentally step on it again, you won't mind?"

He laughed. "Well, I wouldn't go that far. And to answer your question before you stomped my foot— I'm not planning on jumping into marriage. I can do this job single. I still have to talk with Mike and Gladys more and see where they are at. I guess in the morning they will tell me what I need to know when I go out there. Please keep this to yourself. You're actually the first person I've mentioned this to."

Pleasure filled her up, as if she were a glass filling with fresh, sparkling water. She smiled at him and his eyes warmed.

She caught movement out of the corner of her eye and glanced around, only then realizing the music had stopped and people were leaving the designated dance floor while she and Jesse were still dancing. People were watching.

She closed her eyes. "Well, people are watching and we're dancing to no music so I guess we did what you wanted, gave them more to talk about."

A slow smile spread across his face. "I knew it had stopped, but hey, I figured the moment that you realized it stopped, you'd be walking away and we weren't finished talking. You dance pretty smooth for a heiress used to dancing fancy at all these black-tie events you attend all over the country." The man was so aggravating as he so easily brought it all back down to her money. "So you're just letting me stand out here and do this?"

He grinned and leaned close, his warm breath whispered over her ear. "You didn't know it had ended."

She shivered and her ear tingled. She turned her head slightly to stare at him, his dark molten eyes bore into hers. "I'm so going to regret dancing with you. Especially since Granddaddy is watching us, he's got his eyes on you, Jesse James, and I'm probably about to suffer because of it."

The music started to play again. It was a little bit faster but not much; they could still two-step to it, just a little increased speed. And he immediately started moving again.

She stumbled. "Hey, give a girl some warning, would you?"

"What do you mean, he's got his eyes on me?" His tone was as stiff as his jaw.

He was not happy.

* * *

Jesse tried to keep his features neutral as he took in

Caroline's declaration. He studied her beautiful features and was completely loving the feel of her in his arms, using this dance as an excuse to hold her for just a little while to discuss the boys ranch.

They had no business being this close and he knew it, but sometimes his head got crazily mixed up and he did stupid things, like insisting she dance with him. She was a billionaire heiress and she had made a name for herself in her own right, too. It wasn't just being an heiress to who knew how much money—billions, he thought—but she was one smart, talented woman. She did beautiful artwork and had a good heart and a sassy tongue to go with it. And they had been friends for a very long time.

Friends who walked a tightrope because they both knew they were attracted to each other. But a small-town sheriff and a billionaire heiress did not mix. He had put a wall between them, and now they just had this ongoing battle of wills that just hid or helped them work through the undeniable attraction between them.

They wouldn't get along, even if that push and pull wasn't there. At least that's what he told himself. But now he was genuinely disturbed by what she had said.

When she didn't answer, he narrowed his eyes. "Why is he watching me?" His gaze dropped to her flattened lips, and he again tried to hide the crazy desire within him that liked thinking about her marrying him. Liked thinking about kissing her lips once more... It was dangerous for him to think about that.

He had *nothing* to offer her—even if they could get along.

Her eyes narrowed, giving her a very sexy appeal, not something he needed. Involuntarily, his hand flexed on her lower back, spread up as if a caress...as if molding her to himself just ever so much more slightly. He told himself to stop, but sometimes a man just reacted. He fought off the need to hold her even closer. "Why?" he asked once more.

She sighed. "Your name was mentioned in the last family meeting that Granddaddy called. He mentioned you and me, and I think there is a little threat that he has ideas about us."

His boots stuck on the pavement. "You mean he's threatening you with me?"

"There is a firework display that happens most times when you and I are around each other. Because of our interactions, like tonight, people think that we are flirting with attraction. And you egg it on, especially when you stop me all the time."

"I'm law enforcement and you're always breaking

the law. That's all it is. And you know it."

"I know no such thing. You pull me over if I'm doing a mile over the speed limit just to give me a hard time."

He bristled. "You go over the speed limit just to heckle me. You know where I park my SUV most of the time and you always do it anyway. I'm not going to just let that go by, you know."

"And why not?"

"Because it would get around that I'm letting you by with special privileges, and then I'm going to get in trouble with all the other good people of Stonewall. They'll think I'm giving you those special privileges and it's just not a good thing."

She glowered at him now. "Don't tell me you don't let other people off sometimes."

"So we're at an impasse. I'm doing my job and you're breaking the law. We'll drop it at that. Why is your granddaddy thinking that's a good reason we need to get married? And how in the name of thunder is he thinking he's going to do that, anyway? He can't pull my strings."

Irritation coursed through him. Why would her granddaddy think he could do that to him? Nobody owned him. He'd become the sheriff of this town off his reputation and hard work. He prided himself in being a man people looked up to. Nobody owned or manipulated him. And they wouldn't. Not even billionaire Talbert McCoy and this gorgeous woman he knew he would never, ever marry.

"I don't know what makes my granddaddy's mind work. Nor my uncle J.D.'s. I'm not ready for marriage and I told him that already. He doesn't believe me. Anyway, don't worry. I'm not doing what he asked me to do. I can make it on my own and I will. He's got nothing on me."

"Well, that's a good thing to know because I hate to tell you this, sweetheart…we may go way back, but I wouldn't marry you for money."

"Who says I want to marry you anyway? Now, can we get back to talking about the boys ranch?" Fire flashed in her eyes.

"Actually, the song just ended. I was just giving you a heads-up that changes could be on the horizon for the ranch." He forced himself to let her go. His arms felt empty as they dropped away from her and he stepped back.

She looked oddly relieved. "Thank you for letting me know. Now, I think you better think long and hard before you make some kind of crazy decision. Because, to be honest, Jesse, that is a lifetime commitment. I don't know that once you start it you could walk away. Just look at Gladys and Mike. Forty years of endless obstacles to overcome. Fighting the system half the time, fighting for the happiness of boys in need all of the time, and always giving everything you have to help them, to the point of exhaustion. Are you sure you can do that? Full-time?"

Her words hit hard. He snatched his hat from his head and slapped it across his thigh. "I'll do what I have to do to save the ranch. It's all I had at one time in my life. It's all a lot of the boys who are there have. I can't watch it vanish."

With that, he turned and strode across the street, heading toward his truck. He needed to think.

She was right. If that was what it called for, it could change his life forever.

He understood that there was a very good likelihood that once he committed to something this big, this all-consuming, that it might not help his single situation. He might never find a woman to marry him once they realized his responsibility.

Problem was, he was okay with that.

CHAPTER TWO

Jesse parked the truck the next morning out in front of the huge two-story house that he had grown up in. The place was in good shape, thanks to all the donations that came in from people like Caroline and her family and from the guys who had been raised here like him. They had an annual donation drive that gave everyone the chance to pay back some of the good they'd gotten from living here. So money had never been a big issue because of all the people who believed in what the ranch stood for and were so gracious to give.

He strode toward the house and took the four steps in two to reach the wraparound porch of the rambling ranch house. He knocked on the door and waited.

He loved this house and counted everyone living here as his family. He felt a deep sense of protectiveness for them. He hadn't been good enough for his biological parents—they'd abandoned him when he was a very young boy. They'd left him at a bus station, alone, hungry and crying. He closed his eyes, effectively closing the door on thoughts of his past. He didn't like to dwell on his past because there was no changing it. But he'd learned here—at this ranch, under the care and love of Mike and Gladys, who had saved him—that he could only control his future by the choices he made in his own life. For that wisdom and their love, he owed them everything. And that meant even taking over the ranch when the time was right for them to retire.

The door opened and Gladys—short, cute as a bug with her curly gray hair and her big smile—eyed him with a saucy look. She was a fireball but moving slower every day, and that ate at him.

Her smile was big. "Boy, what are you doing? I told you, just come on in. You're making me walk all the way from the kitchen to this front door. If you're not going to come in the house by yourself, at least come to the kitchen where you belong. You know where that back door is."

He laughed. "I know. I should've driven around back. I don't know what I was thinking but I need to get you a big paddle or something. You know that big ole spoon you used to threaten me with when I was growing   up?"

She gave him a hug and patted him on the back. "You know, even if I had used that spoon, it wouldn't have done any good on your raw hide anyway."

"Well, you're right about that."

"Ha. Come on in here. I baked a coffee cake just for you because I knew you were coming—just didn't expect you at the front door."

He removed his hat and followed her into the house and down the hardwood floor to the large kitchen at the back of the house. It smelled like cinnamon and vanilla, the heavenly scent of her coffee cake. His stomach growled. He was glad the boys were all in school or there wouldn't be a crumb left, which made this the perfect time to have a little breakfast meeting. And for him to get a great slice of homemade cake.

Mike came in the back door as they were walking in. He hung up his hat on the hat rack and Jesse hung his beside Mike's. He stared at the two of them for a moment as a small, nostalgic smile played on his lips. Mike had given him a small cowboy hat when he'd first come to the ranch; it had been small but still too big for him. He'd eventually grown into it and then out of it. Now they wore the same size. But like he could never completely fill Mike's shoes, he could never quite fill his hat either. Mike McNealy was a great man among men.

Mike slapped a hand to his shoulder and squeezed. "Good to see you, son."

Even as a man in his late seventies or early eighties—Jesse couldn't remember Mike's exact age—Mike was still a strong, fit man with a big heart. He was a good man who made lost boys into men.

"Did you have fun at the street dance last night?" He smiled and headed toward the kitchen table. Jesse followed him. "It's always a good time. Great crowd. Where were y'all? It was a benefit for the ranch—I assumed y'all would be there."

Mike's gaze shifted away, toward Gladys, then back. "We stayed in. You know, we had to keep an eye on the boys. But we appreciated everything everyone did for the ranch. Haven't heard how much was raised but you know we are always amazed and humbled by everyone's generosity. I also heard you danced several dances with Caroline and then left early."

He narrowed his eyes at Mike. "And just how did you know this?"

The Stonewall grapevine was quite active but he had a feeling he knew who had filled them in. He leveled a knowing gaze on Gladys.

She waved a hand. "Now stop that. Penny called."

Mike grinned. "You know she's going to call Gladys and tell her everything, especially if it has to do with you or one of the other boys."

"Yep, I knew that. But I just thought I'd check— just making sure there weren't any new vines stretching out from that grapevine that I hadn't heard about."

Mike rolled his eyes. "Look no further. Sometimes I feel like we've got a whole vineyard growing here in this kitchen. When that phone starts ringing, Gladys can sound like a whole brood of hens by herself when she's talking. I swear, sometimes I think she's got multiple phones to each ear."

Jesse sat down at the bar and cupped his hands together, feeling right at home with the teasing that went on between Gladys and Mike.

Gladys eyed him from across the room while she filled coffee cups. She held an empty mug up. "You watch your mouth, Mike, or I won't give you any of this coffee. And I won't give you any of this coffee cake. You don't need it, anyway."

Mike patted his flat gut. "I will welcome it to grow. At my age, I deserve to have a gut. But keeping up with a herd of boys for as long as I have and running this ranch won't let it grow. Even with your great cooking."

It was true. Mike was probably the healthiest man alive for his age. Jesse needed to keep that in mind as he tried to stay healthy himself.

Gladys set a coffee cup in front of him, then one in front of Mike and kissed his temple. "I like your flat gut. But I would love you if it wasn't."

"You are the woman of my heart, Gladys McNealy."

"Right answer." She chuckled and then looked at Jesse. "Jesse James, you need to put a ring on some good woman's finger and have what Mike and I have…you know you want it."

"Now, Gladys, don't start all that. You know I'm not the marrying kind."

Mike grimaced. "Don't tell her that—you know she'll get started again."

She tended to give him an earful when he said things like that. She wanted her boys married, and she wanted them married fast. And she wanted grandbabies. She didn't have any kids of her own, but she counted every boy who had come through the ranch as one of her boys, and their kids as her grandbabies, and they loved it. He just wasn't sure he'd be the one to give her one. He just didn't see any way past his dilemma, to do what she asked.

She set the coffee cake down in front of him and then put her hands on her hips. "You know, that Caroline is getting more beautiful every day."

He frowned. "Gladys, don't start on Caroline. There is nothing there. I know everybody thinks there is, but there is nothing there. She and I would scratch each other's eyes out. Y'all think you're seeing fireworks but that's not what you're seeing." He cringed at the white lie, but he didn't know what else to do—never had.

Gladys sat down on her stool, took the knife, and cut the coffee cake. She placed the pieces on three plates and then passed them around. Finally, she spoke. "You know I love you, Jesse James. You know I know when you're fibbing. But I'm going to let this slide because I know it's a private war that you have waged within yourself. I'm just not sure how to overcome this."

And there it was: Gladys believed that he was not telling the truth about how he felt about Caroline, and he would never let on that she was right. "This is delicious." He stuffed a piece in his mouth, telling her it was delicious before he had even taken a bite just because he knew it would be delicious.

She chuckled. "One of these days, I'm going to make a terrible one so that when you tell me that and then take a bite. you'll cough or something because it will be awful."

He grinned as he chewed. "That would be funny. I don't think you could make a bad pie or cake even if you tried—though you couldn't allow yourself to do that."

She sighed. "You're probably right."

Mike didn't pick up his fork. Instead, he picked up his coffee mug. His eyes were serious as they met Jesse's over the rim as he took a drink. Jesse watched him set the mug down and knew he was finally about to hear what was bothering his mentor.

"All right, let's talk turkey," Mike said.

"I'd like that."

"As much as we hate it, we need...I mean, we're ready to retire."

Gladys suddenly looked fidgety and her face paled.

He set his fork down. "Good for you. You two deserve it. And I can have everything in place to take over as soon as you say the word. We just need to get the paperwork done." He was relieved that they'd finally decided to do this. He'd been treading water for two years, waiting for them to decide. He'd been thinking something else was wrong, so this was a relief. "When is the date? I'll get everything ready.

I've always loved this place. And its mission."

Mike cupped his hands together and leveled serious gray eyes on him. "We understand that, and we appreciate it. And we want you to take over because we do believe you are the right man for the job. *And* the guys love you. They respect you, and we feel like you would be the perfect man to carry on this wonderful and amazing legacy that we've been able to create here. But…" He cleared his throat and Jesse's gut tightened. "There's a stipulation that we haven't mentioned to you before, because we thought when the time came, it wouldn't be relevant. But though we've waited two years for you, you never have…"

"Never have what?"

"Gotten married." Mike gave him a measured stare. "To take over this place, you have to be married."

Gladys had turned pink and stared at her coffee.

Jesse's skin turned hot as Mike's words settled over him. "I have to be *married*? Why did you guys not tell me this?" They both stared at him apologetically. "As you can clearly see, I am not married. And what's this about—y'all have been waiting?" His slow-to-anger temper had skyrocketed. This was important, and they hadn't thought in all the time they'd been discussing this over the last couple of years to mention it to him until it was down to the wire?

"Jesse." Gladys reached out to pat his arm and to push his coffee cake a little closer to him. "We were just thinking that you would find one of these young ladies especially nice and you would settle down and get married. And then we would make a decision on what would happen. But you haven't." She sighed. "So now we have to just come out and tell you. If you want this place, if you want to be the mentor to all these young boys who really and truly do need you…then, Jesse James, you have to get married. And that's all there is to it. Somehow in the next two months even—"

"What do you mean—*two* months?" He stared from one to the other. "Now me getting married has a timeline." He narrowed his gaze. This was too fishy. "Is there something else I don't know about? I'm genuinely confused here. Out with it. I need straight answers. What is going on?"

Mike cupped his hands together. "I'm having some health issues. The doctor has told me that I have to slow down. My blood pressure has been going up lately, and I'm having heart fluctuations that are being monitored."

"How serious?" Alarm rang through him.

"My ticker is finally giving me some trouble, family history that I thought I'd missed. Kind of runs in my family. My dad died of it, my uncle died of it, and well, it's caught up with me. And to be honest, it's worrying Gladys to pieces. So that's part of why we finally couldn't wait on you any longer."

Jesse was gripped by concern for his foster dad. "Mike, you should have told me. You know I'm there for you and I'm sorry—I'm sorry you didn't tell me and I'm sorry you're having to go through this. You look like the healthiest man your age I've ever seen."

"The exterior doesn't tell the whole story. Family history will get you sometimes. But I'm being proactive here now. We are stepping down, one way or the other. I just hope we don't have to—"

"Stop." Jesse stared at the two people he loved more than anything in the world. "You won't have to think about that last choice. Let me do some research today and I'll figure this out. I'm going to take care of this. You can count on me." He'd make sure of that.

* * *

Saturday morning Caroline stared at the house that she had been raised in after her mother and dad, along with her aunt and uncle, had been killed in a private plane crash on their way back from a Vegas horse show.

She tapped her red shoe on the stone walkway and tried to calm her racing heart.

Her granddaddy and grandmother had taken them in, loved them through their grief and given them a safe place to land. She owed him so much. And she loved him, loved him more than life itself. But that didn't mean he was going to push her around.

No, he was not, and he knew it too.

She had made it clear the last two meetings they'd had with all the family gathered over the last few months that although he had set the ultimatums for her brothers Ash and Denton, she was not going to be happy if he tried to force her to marry someone, especially Jesse James. Whom he had mentioned. She and Jesse James were not a match. There were fireworks when they were close together and there was that attraction that could not be denied, but they were both smart adults who thought it was not a good idea. They would be combustible—and not in a good way.

Nope, she was sure and certain that Jesse James would run as fast as he could if her granddaddy tried to force him to marry her. And how embarrassing was that? No way.

Taking a deep breath, she mentally pulled up her big girl panties and opened the front door, not the side door she usually used—she was going in, all guns blazing. Her granddaddy was one strong-willed fella and used to always getting his way. In business and at home. He had a reputation for being a good man, but hard-core when it was something he believed in. It was hard to deny the guy. But today she was denying him by defying him.

Ash and Denton, for some reason, had ended up jumping on board and giving him exactly what he wanted on a silver platter. Now her granddaddy thought she was going to be that easy.

Wrong.

The spiked heels of her most expensive shoes clacked on the terrazzo as she strode down the hallway toward the huge oak doors that led into Granddaddy's office. She was late. She had done that on purpose. She knew she was making her granddaddy and all her brothers wait on her. But so be it. She knew from the look on her granddaddy's face last night at the dance that this meeting had been called for her.

She flung open the door and four sets of eyes landed on her.

Hiking her nose in the air, she shook her long mane of blonde hair and leveled a gaze at Granddaddy. "We can just cut to the chase because I know what's coming and I know I'm telling you right now—no."

Talbert McCoy was a handsome man even at his age, especially when he smiled. He smiled now. He loved a challenge and she had just laid down the gauntlet.

"Come in, darlin'. Have a seat. I saved one right here in the front row for you."

She eyed her brothers, who were all watching with barely concealed mirth. All but Beck, who, like her, found nothing about this funny. He was next and knew it.

When she didn't move, Talbert added, "You can stand there all you want, but you might as well come get comfortable."

If she continued to stand, he would think she was weak, scared of sitting and ready to bolt. So, with her spine stiff and her shoulders back, she strode to the chair that was waiting for her beside Denton and sat down. Her brother, country singer superstar that he was turning into, was slouched to the side with his ankle crossed over one knee and his hat cocked back as he watched her. That stinking, cocky grin of his was wide. The good-looking devil was having more fun watching her. He knew exactly what she was going through, and yet because he had fallen in love with Blaze, he was enjoying watching her suffer.

She shot him a look that told him exactly what she

thought of him—he shot a wink back at her. "Come on, little sister. *Love* is a wondrous thing."

"Not when you're being forced." She shot Granddaddy a glare. "And I'm not marrying Jesse James."

Across the room, Ash's chuckle drew her attention. He watched with twinkling eyes. And why not? Like Denton, he was extremely happily married now *and* expecting his first baby.

"Denton's right. I understand you don't want to marry Jesse James, and that's between you and Granddaddy. But I have to be honest and tell you I'm probably the happiest man on earth right now, and I have a little bit of that to thank from Granddaddy right there."

Denton sat up. "Hold on, now—I'm the happiest man alive."

They both laughed.

"Cut it out. You are not helping my situation," she snapped and shot Beck a glance, thinking he might give her a little help.

He leaned against the mantel of the fireplace, his well-defined arms crossed as he watched them. He shook his head, frustration in his expression. He was ready to walk out the door and keep on going. Clearly his patience had run out.

Hers, too. She faced her granddaddy. He was smiling; he always had thought her temper was funny. It was aggravating.

Talbert leaned back in his leather chair. "My four favorite people in all the world. I'm glad to see you. Ash and Denton—I'm happy y'all are so happy with your sweet brides. And I'm glad I had a little part in your joy. Ash, I can't wait to hold my new great-grandbaby in my arms, and I love little Tess with all my heart. Denton, I'm looking forward to when you and Blaze give me a great-grandbaby. It's going to be a great day."

His joy was clear and she struggled momentarily to not fall for his joy. Listening to him, one could forget that he'd forced them to marry or else lose their inheritance. It was wrong.

His gaze landed on her. "And now, my sweet Caroline. I saw you and Jesse James last night. You two have been dancing around each other for years and last night y'all were dancing pretty close. Y'all were having a really close conversation, with him whispering in your ear. I thought he was going to kiss you right there on the dance floor. My heart pumped faster with excitement for you, little girl." She stiffened. "I am not a little girl and I am not your sweet Caroline—not right now, anyway."

"You always will be my little girl and my sweet Caroline. But I've been warning you this was coming. And I've decided that since you've known this was coming, your time will start when you walk out that door."

"What?" She stared at him, shocked. Everybody else had gotten a little bit of warning. "I've locked down your inheritance already. I know there are a few things going on out there, and you're going to want to be able to give a helping hand to all those charities you love, and I love too. It hurts my heart to do this, but it's the only way I see to get you to cooperate. In order to unlock your inheritance and your other accounts and help your beloved charities, you're going to have to marry Jesse James. And do it within the next two months and stay married for three months—or you lose it all. I've pulled a few strings with people I know and you're not going to get any more art shows until you marry him. I'm having to do a bit of hard-core intervention for you. I was hoping I wouldn't have to do that but you are one stubborn woman."

"I take after you, so don't hold your breath that I'm going to do this."

He chuckled. "Yes, you do take after me, and yes, you will do it. I have to have hope that maybe this will be what will work for you and Jesse James since you two just don't seem to understand that y'all were made for each other."

She dropped her forehead to her palm. *He was cutting off her charities.*

She had been born into all this money and had realized as a teenager the value of what she could do with her money and with her philanthropy. Everyone teased her because she loved to shop, and she did. She had a true love for beautiful shoes and spa days. She wasn't perfect and right now the feel of her designer shoes gave her little comfort. She stood, tall and proud and unwilling to let him see how shaken she was that he had done this. She stared at Granddaddy. Her heart thundered.

"Why—why would you punish the charities? And your own philanthropy, too? It's just wrong. And I'm highly, highly disappointed in you, Granddaddy. Of all the things that you could ask me to do or force upon me, hurting innocent people who count on this money and these charities…I am floored and completely torn up."

The room was silent and for a moment, Talbert McCoy looked shaken. And that told her just how hard this was for him. Did he want great-grandchildren that bad that he would do this?

"Caroline, I know this is hard. But when I took

you and your brothers on after your parents died, I promised myself and I promised your grandma that I would see you happy. Happy and fulfilled and thriving. And I waited, and I watched, just like I did with your brothers. But my sweet girl, you're different. You have just thrown yourself into these charities and helping others. You wander around here shopping, and yes, brightening everybody's day who you come in contact with because you are such a good, loving, and spirited person. But that's not the life I promised or vowed that I would give to you. And every time I visit your daddy's, mother's, and grandmother's graves, I'm reminded that I vowed that I would see you happy and thriving and fulfilled…and you're not. A pair of fancy high-heeled shoes is not the same as holding a baby in your arms and having the love of a good man in your life. And that's why I'm doing this."

She told her feet to move but they were planted to the ground as she and her Granddaddy's gazes held.

"I have to say also that people are concerned about Jesse James, too. We've all watched you and him, and it's like the world doesn't exist when you are near each other. I have never seen as much promise as I see sparking between the two of you. I wish you'd trust me. But even if you don't, this is it. When you walk out that door, my sweet girl, everything's cut off.

You've got one credit card that's going to work—but it's got a low credit amount on it. And all your other bank accounts are froze up. And I believe that Jesse James is the answer. I believe that when you tell him the ultimatum, that he's crazy enough about you— whether you believe it or not—that he'll jump right on board to help you. All I'm asking is the two of you spend three months married to give yourselves a shot at happiness. I believe with all my heart and soul this is the most exciting and rewarding union that you could ever imagine. You two have the ability to change many lives. When I took you four kids into this house after we lost your parents, I can tell you that touching lives in a personal way is the best reward that God ever gave us on this earth."

His gaze bore into her and a shiver raced through her. He'd taken the wind out of her. Caroline couldn't move. She could barely breathe. Her brothers had gone silent. Her granddaddy had just laid his heart out there and she loved him with all of her heart.

But this was still wrong.

Yet he had been telling the truth, the truth that had hit her years ago when she'd started pumping funds into the boys' ranch and other causes she believed in. If it hadn't been for him and her grandmother—and if not them, then her uncle J.D.—who would have taken her and her brothers in after they lost their mom and dad in that horrible tragedy? They would have been left alone, needing help…like the boys at the ranch. She'd been living her whole life to touch lives like her granddaddy had done. And she'd been doing it through her philanthropy.

And now she knew. He was talking about her and Jesse and the boys home. Her granddaddy knew that the boys home was in some kind of trouble.

Her legs were wobbly, but she tried to appear stable. She had a view of her face in the mantel mirror; she glanced over and saw Beck, his face impassive as he, too, saw how pale she was. Her brothers all watched quietly. But they were letting this play out between her and Granddaddy because they knew that this was her time. Her time to handle it her way.

"I'm not sure what I'm about to do other than walk out that door, Granddaddy. I'll make my decision later. But I do know that unless something drastic happens, I'm not going to be walking back through that door. I love you, but this time you've gone too far. I hope that it's worth it to you."

With that, she turned and strode on determined feet out the door and let it swing closed behind her.

CHAPTER THREE

Beck had been startled and angered by what had just happened. He respected his sister very much and he knew that his decision would be the same as hers. He was already lining his stuff up because he knew that when his granddaddy laid down the gauntlet, he was going to walk away. He loved his charter plane business, but he knew that his granddaddy was going to have him over a barrel, because he owned a slight majority of his company. He knew what was coming down the pass for him, especially after watching his granddaddy be so ruthless with Caroline—his only granddaughter, who had always had him wrapped around her little finger.

He studied his granddaddy and could see that though certain of his plan, he was still shaken by her exit. He covered it quickly.

Beck stepped forward. "Have you factored Jesse into this? He is not one to be led around by the nose. He won't marry Caroline just because you want him to. Yeah, I agree there's fireworks between them but they're pretty combustible. The two of them might kill each other if they have to be married for three months. I'm just thinking on this one, you might have misjudged my sister and Jesse."

Talbert leveled him with a softened gaze. "Beck, I've told you before and I'll tell you again—sometimes love comes out in weird ways. Your sister is floundering. Maybe she doesn't know it, but I see it and I can't just not give this a shot. And like I said, it is a little bit selfish on my part because I want to see y'all happy and I want great-grandbabies. So, take it for what you want but that's the way it stands. Now, I assume you're preparing for what I have in store for you. Just remember I love you and it's going to be all right."

Beck almost laughed. Almost.

Instead, he stared from beneath the brim of his hat at Ash and Denton, who watched with bemused expressions. He knew when they left the room they'd probably give him a hard time, teasing him like brothers normally did. But right now, he wasn't in the mood for any of it. He followed Caroline out the door.

He still had a jet charter business to run. He figured he had little more than three months to come up with a plan or to lose everything he'd worked for.

* * *

Caroline felt the need for speed. She stomped out of the house and got into her BMW, put it in reverse and backed out of the drive, spinning her tires as she went. It was childish, she knew, but she just thought better when she had speed going. This was all too crazy.

She stomped the gas and headed out the long drive of the McCoy ranch. The convertible's top was down and the wind helped relieve the heat burning through her skin from the inside out.

When she turned onto the country road, she floored the gas pedal, glad it was a straight road for a long way. Her eyes stung…from the wind in her eyes. Her heart hurt and her stomach churned as the air streamed through her hair. Normally this calmed her spirits but not today. Nothing could do that…she would not cry. She would not.

She would figure out a plan of action and then take that action.

She thought best with the top down on her little red car and the wind in her face.

Marry Jesse.

It was ridiculous.

Still, it was a secret, heartfelt deep-down wish that could never happen.

Could never work.

Thoughts and regrets spun through her head as the miles ticked by rapidly. The straightaway ended with a curve that she took faster than was safe and it was then and only then that she realized where she was as she pulled her foot from the gas pedal.

Too late, lights flashed in her rearview and she groaned. *Jesse.* He had been sitting back there, right behind that bush, where he seemed to spend half his time just to torment her since she had to drive this way from the ranch. Knowing this, she usually sped here just to irritate him. But she hadn't been thinking about him being there today and she had been going too fast.

Dangerously fast.

He was going to be furious. She pressed the brake and slowed down as she eased to the side of the road. This was a good thing; she needed to tell him what was going on. After all, he was a part of this equation. And he was going to be just as unhappy as she was. If Granddaddy thought he was going to go along with this little scheme of his like a sheep to the slaughterhouse, he was wrong. Jesse did not want to get married. Most especially to her.

The man had commitment issues and more than that going on when it came to her.

She had thought at one point that he might marry one of his girlfriends but then she realized that he had commitment issues. Big-time commitment issues. And there had been a time, before she talked herself into realizing that they would never make a couple, that she had believed she was the woman who could change his mind about commitment—then she'd learned that that was never going to happen.

Her having money bothered the heck out of him. It didn't dawn on her until she saw him in the rearview slowly get out of the vehicle, that she was one broke female.

For the first time in their lives, he might actually want her.

Ha, even that didn't make her feel better.

As he stopped at the car she mustered up her sarcastic side and tugged her sunglasses down. "Well, afternoon, Jesse James. How's it going? Fancy seeing you here on this beautiful sunny day."

He did not smile. "Caroline, you were going twenty miles over the speed limit. You were going nearly eighty miles per hour on a curve. What are you thinking? I'm fixin' to pretty much drag you out of that car and haul you into the jailhouse. How many times do I have to tell you to slow it down? But honestly—" He studied her. "What's up? Why are you so pale?"

"Why are you so irritating? I had a reason for going so fast. Had a bee in my car."

"Try something new—that's an old one."

"I had things on my mind." "Well, if you want to know the truth, I had things on my mind, too. But I was not expecting you to blow by like that. What's wrong?"

She took a deep breath. "Officer, can I get out of the car, please? Do I have your permission?"

He pulled his shades off so she could see his hard expression, then he pocketed the sunshades and stepped back. "Yes, ma'am. You may get out then move over by the grass."

She got out slowly, her high heels not liking the gravel. As she stood, her ankles wobbled and three uncertain steps from the car, she stumbled.

And of course, Jesse caught her.

Her hand slammed against his hard chest as his arms went around her waist and he pulled her to him. She tried to help her situation so she could step away from him. No luck; her legs suddenly seemed to be liquid when their gazes met and held.

This man was rugged and about the most gorgeous

man she had ever seen. Her pulse raced as his dark eyes seemed to see every corner of her soul. Her heart sighed with want.

She tried to gather her wits. "I guess you're going to have to help me since these shoes are not cooperating on the gravel."

His gaze dropped to her lips and her pulse skyrocketed.

"You know, I don't understand why you wear those shoes in the first place," he said, with a huskiness to his voice that gave her goose bumps. "I mean, I can see it if you're going to New York or something, but around here, those things can get you hurt."

Despite lecturing her, he didn't move but continued to support her with his arms. She could feel his heart pounding too. "Jesse James, are you going to lecture me about my shoes or are you going to help me get to the tailgate of that police vehicle of yours?"

"I'm assuming if you're wanting me to take my tailgate down, you're having some kind of problem you need to talk to me about?"

"Yes, Jesse." She sighed. "We need to talk."

He looked heavenward and for a moment, she thought she saw something like sadness flicker in his eyes. But he looked back at her, looking just irritated. "Come on, walk with me." He held her close with one arm and her snug up against his hip as he practically carried her with her feet dangling across the gravel. He looked highly irritated at the whole experience. When they reached his tailgate, using one hand, he unhooked the latch and lowered the tailgate. Then, he wrapped both of his big, capable hands around her waist and lifted her up and set her on it.

She tugged at her skirt and tried very hard not to miss the feel of his hands on her waist.

He stepped one step back and put his hands on his hips. "What's up?"

He was going to have a coronary when he found out that her granddaddy expected him to marry her in order to save her inheritance—which he needed for the boys ranch if it was in trouble. He needed her cash.

The truth was he needed her. As much as he hated her money, when it came to the boys ranch, he loved it. And what was new about that? It all boiled down to any man she dated, there was that money issue always getting in her way of being a normal human being. But she wasn't going to let that sob story get a hold on her. Like she always said, she was grateful to have it and to be able to use it to help others. She bit her lip, knowing it all depended on him.

His hat shadowed his eyes as he stared at her. He *did* make a gorgeous sheriff.

Get a grip.

"Well, you going to talk?"

"Don't rush me. It's important, and you're not going to like it. I didn't like it myself when I heard it. But remember I warned you last night that Granddaddy was watching?"

"And?"

"I got the verdict this morning. It's my turn."

"What do you mean?"

"Granddaddy is trying to force me to get married, just like he's done with Ash and Denton."

"So, it's true? They had to get married or lose their inheritance?"

She nodded. "Sad but true. See, I had a really good reason to speed and blow off steam. I think after I tell you the news, you may hop into this vehicle and speed too."

His brows dipped. "After the morning I've had, I'm tempted to do it anyway."

"Is something wrong?"

"Yeah, I think I need to sit on the tailgate too."

Concerned, she watched him turn and scoot onto the tailgate. He sat with his legs spread slightly, his knee pressed against hers.

"We have a problem, deeper than you know."

"What's wrong?"

"Mike is having health issues. His heart's acting up on him and his blood pressure is high. He's having tests run. He could have a stroke or a heart attack—he told me a little bit ago and it blindsided me. I've been sitting here trying to figure out what I need to do. I guess I took it for granted—he looked so healthy, you know?"

Unable to stop herself, she put her hand on his arm, trying to comfort him. She knew how much he cared for Mike and Gladys. "I'm so sorry. And Gladys, how's   she?"
"Worried and trying to hide how much. She's so used to hiding if she's worried. You know, if you're raising that many boys, the woman has spent a lot of time on her knees praying and hiding her worry behind closed doors. She didn't succeed this morning."

His mouth formed a straight, grim line and he hung his head for a minute. Caroline rubbed his arm, wanting to give him some kind of comfort. Her heart went out to him. Jesse's parents had abandoned him at a bus station. The very thought of it always made her angry. There was no excuse for it. Even if they were desperate, they should have put him somewhere safe, not a public bus station at his young age, where anyone could have grabbed him. Thankfully, somebody had rescued him, wandering around, alone and hungry and distraught. The thought of him like that tore her up. And seeing his worry now wasn't easy either, considering he was the town's rock.

Emotions swamped her, and she was not an emotional woman. After her mom and daddy's funeral, she had pretty much locked away the tears. But now, looking at Jesse and knowing that he was so worried, and probably because she was in such turmoil herself, tears threatened.

Suck it up, buttercup.

She sniffed.

"Are you okay?"

"I'm worried about him, too. I can sniff."

"Yeah. I know you just don't cry normally."

"Well, take a good look now because after about five minutes, you won't see it again. But is it, I mean, is he going to be okay? Please, fill me in."

"The doctor told him he needs to slow down. Let go of some stress. I'm worried, too."

Her own troubles faded in the face of worrying about Mike. Her hand lingered on Jesse's arm. Her thumb caressed gently back and forth, needing to comfort him. "I understand. What are they going to do?"

"They're going to walk away if nobody can take over the ranch and the boys."

This very statement told her how serious this was. "Aren't you planning to do that?"

He got a strange look on his face. "I was. But, Caroline, there's a problem."

"And what is that?"

"I can't take over the boys ranch."

Her hand dropped to her lap. "What do you mean, you can't? You're a law enforcement officer and the most capable man in the world to take over. And the boys adore you. They respect you. You're exactly what those boys need. And you want to do this. I'm confused."

Their gazes drilled into each other.

She was suddenly leery. Something didn't feel right. She groaned. "Tell me what's going on."

"There is suddenly a stipulation that I have to be married in order to take over the ranch."

She gasped. All the breath left her body and she felt dizzy, as if she were a deflating balloon flying crazily all over the place, banging up against everything until it fell flat on the floor, completely deflated.

She tried to swallow, tried to suck in some breath, to get her bearings. "Who wrote that stipulation? Has the whole world just gone crazy? I've never heard of people having to get married to save things, but suddenly you and me both have to get married—" She closed her eyes, leaned her head back, and let the sun warm her cold face. "Granddaddy."

"Why would he do that?"

She sighed. "Because, he's doing it to me and you because in order to save my inheritance, I have to marry you. And this stipulation that suddenly shows up at the ranch is his way of forcing us to get married. What Talbert McCoy wants Talbert McCoy gets. Obviously, he's more ruthless than I ever imagined."

"He's trying to force you to marry me?" Jesse stood, yanked his hat off, and slapped it across his thigh. "Mike and Gladys would not lie to me about this, and I don't believe they would conspire to trap me into marrying you."

His words stabbed at her. "Okay, that was a little hard blow. So, I'm a trap?"

"You know what I mean. We're both being trapped. You don't want to marry me, and I don't want to marry you. And I'm not going to marry you, just so you know. We would hurt each other. You would drive me crazy. I could put up with you for a little while, but you know you're ornery and selfish—"

"I am not selfish. All you ever have to do is call me and you know I'll give you whatever you need except…"

"I don't want *that*, just so you know."

"I don't want kisses from you either. And it was your fault anyway."

"It was a huge mistake and we were both guilty, so don't start on me that it was all my fault. You jumped into that kiss as much as I did." He took a deep breath and stepped back from her.

She crossed her arms. "I'm not going to launch myself at you, so you don't need to keep backing up." He'd opened the past and her mind had gone back to the moment a year ago when they'd both lost their minds and let their bantering get out of hand, and he'd kissed her. Long, passionate, and so amazingly that she could never let herself think about it because it hurt too much, longing for something so much and knowing he didn't want her.

After it had happened, they were pretty much at each other's throats all the time. But that was just because it had been an amazing kiss and even though she had wanted more, the hard-headed cowboy didn't like her money. It still hurt. It wasn't as though there was something she could do about that; she'd been born with it. It would always be between them.

Except right now.

"If you aren't going to get married in order to save the boys ranch, then what are you going to do?"

"I'm going to get to the truth. And then figure out how to fix this and take over the ranch without being forced into marriage."

"My granddaddy believes that he's doing me and you a big favor. And as misguided as that is, that is what's motivating him. If Mike told him about his situation, I have a feeling that Granddaddy might have convinced them that this was best for you too. You know how persuasive he is."

He shook his head, turned his back on her, and strode down the side of the road.

She watched him. The man had a swagger that was just mesmerizing and not something she needed to be thinking about. He paced when he was thinking, and she needed to be thinking, too. Because they were in a no-win situation.

CHAPTER FOUR

Jesse strode down the side of the country road as his mind shuffled through everything Caroline had said, but something wasn't ringing true.

He headed back to where she sat on the tailgate, watching him with a troubled expression. She was so beautiful—and a thorn in his side, always had been. And now her granddaddy was a thorn in his other side. The thought that Talbert would force her to get married at all was disturbing, and even more that he was trying to force her to marry him was too much.

And he and Jesse would have a meeting of the minds about it.

Still, something wasn't right. Caroline was leaving something out. He reached her and those big eyes of hers melted his insides, and he found himself wanting to kiss her lips like they were strawberry jelly on toast.

Yeah, he was hungry; he hadn't eaten but a couple of forkfuls of Gladys's amazing coffee cake before he'd stormed out of the ranch house.

"Okay, come clean. What are you not telling me? There has to be more to your granddaddy trying to force you to marry me. What's he holding over you?"

Her expression fell. "Okay, it's the boys ranch. It's all my charities, my foundations that I care about. He's taken all of my inheritance—put a hold on all of it as of an hour ago. I have two months to marry you or it's all gone. Don't you understand what this means to me? I can live without my fancy shoes and my spa trips and shopping. As of an hour ago, all my philanthropy is dried up. None of the organizations I love and support are getting any money from my closed accounts. And he has stopped supporting them, too. That's what he's got on me. As of an hour ago, I have nothing to offer anyone."

That was not what he expected. He had not thought that Talbert would hold out on the charities that depended on him, the causes that depended on him—especially the boys ranch. These boys lived around here and the older guys worked sometimes as ranch hands on the surrounding ranches. Talbert knew these boys and had always been good at hiring them to teach them how to work cattle. And now he was cutting the ranch off.

"Wow. He's lost his mind."

Pain crossed her face. "I know. I'm so frustrated. So sad." She hopped from the tailgate and started forward—he figured to pace like he had done. However, the instant her spiked heels hit the rocks, her ankles wobbled. "Oh," she gasped, starting to crumble.

He moved fast, catching her against his chest before she landed on her pretty rear. "Gotcha. Those shoes are going to be the death of you." He was starting to like holding her this close far too much.

"You might be right. I'll take them off." Her eyes grew troubled. "And I'll live through this, so you don't have to worry about marrying me. You figure your problem out and I'll figure mine out." Defiance filled her eyes and sounded in her tone.

His gut twisted at the hurt he saw hidden behind that defiance. He fought liking that she felt right in his arms. He couldn't let himself think about that because there was too much padding between them, and by that he meant greenbacks—money. She might not have it now but if he married her, it would be there again.

"Put me down. I'm ready to leave so I can try to figure out my life going forward."

Guilt sliced through him. "You'll just fall on those shoes."

He slipped an arm under her knees and scooped her up then carried her to her car. "Nope, don't tell me to put you down. I'll do it once we reach your car."

Once he reached it, he set her on her feet next to her car door. It took a lot of effort on his part to let her go. "What are we going to do?"

She swallowed hard. "I'm not sure yet what I'm going to do but rest assured, I'm not marrying you. I may be broke, but I am not being forced into marrying you. I'll find a way to raise money to support the foundations I care about. So there, you should be satisfied." She opened her car door and slid into her car. Her skirt rode up exposing more of her long legs.

He had no answer to her words, though his gut knotted. "You might need to put some ice on that ankle, you twisted it so much today."

She gave him a tight lip smile. "Right. I'll probably do that."

He felt like a buffoon. "Let's both see what we can do to find a way out of all of this."

"I'm pretty sure Granddaddy didn't leave a loophole anywhere and there's not going to be an out. Other than me just walking away. And I do mean walking away. After what he's done, I won't be staying here."

She pushed the start button on her car then put it

in gear.

Panic struck him like a mule kick to the gut. The thought of her leaving Stonewall rankled him as he stepped back. He needed to say something. But what? His heart was pounding in his ears. *Tell her not to leave.*

"Good luck." She shot him a frown, then pulled onto the road and drove away.

He watched her until her car disappeared in the distance. He had to figure something out.

* * *

Caroline spent the rest of the weekend calling all her financial people and interrupting their days off to learn she was locked out of everything. There was no getting out of it.

By Thursday evening, she sat on the couch biting her lower lip and feeling pretty low and oh so terribly embarrassed. How could she have let this happen?

She had failed herself in so many ways.

Her phone rang and she picked it up. It was Ginny, married to her cousin Todd. They got along well; they were kind of alike in many ways. She pushed the Accept button. Instantly, Ginny's face came on the screen.

"Okay, girlfriend, I'm hot. I just heard what your granddaddy did, and I have to tell you I think of all these things, this is just way, way too much. Todd was at the clinic this morning with our puppy, and Ash told him the news. Said you were upset. He said Granddaddy really did a number on you and told him all about it. I know you, and I know you're hot."

"To say the least. Ginny, I'm feeling pretty low right now. I've never felt low like this. Just feeling stupid. I've never realized how much control he had over my accounts. Here I thought I was an independent woman. What a joke...turns out I am totally not. What I am is a freeloader, still living in his pool house. I've been basically bumming." She closed her eyes as the truth, so harsh and true kicked her in the gut again. "I mean, yeah, I've been making money, just clicking along thinking I was all that, doing my thing, and come to find out all my accounts are just still connected to him. See, subconsciously, that means I was scared that if I disconnected from him, I'd fall flat on my face." She felt a sob welling inside of her and she blinked hard to keep the tears at bay and hopefully the sob. She could not give into this pity party. No one could know the true depth of her self-loathing right now.

"No, it doesn't. You're being too hard on yourself."

"I'm not. I'm getting real. I was afraid to be on my own. I was really, truly afraid to stick my neck out there and disconnect from him. True, nobody advised me that I needed to disconnect but I'm not stupid. So subconsciously, I let myself get into this mess. And I'm just sick about it. And I'm angry as much at myself as with Granddaddy."

Ginny tilted her yellow cowboy-hatted head to the side and squinted at her through the phone. "You know you are crazy about that sheriff. Don't deny it. I know it and so does everyone else. You are over the moon about him. Why don't you give the two of you a chance?"

"It's not that easy. He has a problem with my money. And I'm not sure if that's all of it. He obviously has commitment issues. You've seen him dating but nothing ever comes of it. He can't commit."

"Maybe the right woman hasn't come along. Or he hasn't figured out that you are more than your money."

She got depressed thinking about that. "Granddaddy even took advantage of the fact that Gladys and Mike want to retire because of his health issues and got them in on his plan, too. They've told Jesse he can't take over unless he's married. But he doesn't want to marry me, therefore I don't want to marry him. I won't beg for anybody's love." Had she really just said that? "I mean, attention. But, it hurts me so bad to know that if the ranch doesn't get the money that keeps them running month to month, they could be in trouble. Jesse didn't mention that and may not know it, but I'm really concerned about their future. If the boys ranch gets into trouble, Granddaddy is responsible. He knows exactly how much they depend on our contributions."

"So, marry Jesse. Take control of this situation. You're strong—you can do this. You've got to stay married for three measly months and after you get your money, you two can go your separate ways and do whatever you want. Turn the tables on him. Quit fighting like he's expecting you to do and go all in. And do it now and get those three months started. Afterward, you two can split up, if you both live through it. Then he'll have his ranch and you can then completely disconnect from your granddaddy. You'll have gotten exactly what you wanted—a new start— and left him with nothing but seeing your back as you walked out the door. That appeals to you, doesn't it?"

It sounded really harsh, but this was what Granddaddy had driven her to. "You're right. But it makes me sad, because I love my granddaddy. But he's gone too far."

"You know, you're in kind of my situation. When

my mom and dad decided to sell my little winery there in Tyler, it hurt, but I did what I had to in order to survive and that was marrying Todd. And it's been a blessing. Anyway, take charge, girlfriend, and if you need us, come over here and we'll call a girls' meeting. We'll meet tomorrow if you want."

Caroline sat there, letting Ginny's words sink in. Her cure for anything had always been a trip to the spa or a shopping spree.

Her stomach felt sick. "Ginny, thank you for your support. You've helped shake me out of my self-pity. I don't even think going to the spa or going shopping would help me, but you're right, I'm strong and I am going to take control. Thanks. Your advice is well taken. Hugs to you. Give that handsome cousin of mine a hug, too. I've got to go."

She pushed the Disconnect button with a forceful jab. *Ginny was right.* She needed to convince Jesse to marry her so they could both get what they wanted when the three months was over. Up to this point, she'd been fooling herself about being strong and independent but no more. She was about to take charge of this situation and she was going to come out of it with her money and her pride. Three months was not that long.

She just had to convince Jesse to play along.

CHAPTER FIVE

Monday afternoon, Jesse drove out to the boys ranch and waved at Greg and Tony, two of the high school kids. They were unloading square bales off the back of a truck into the hay barn. Robbie, one of the first graders, sat on the front porch with a notebook. He pushed his glasses up from where they'd slid a bit down the bridge of his nose and studied Jesse through the thick lenses.

"Hi, Jesse. I'm doing my math. What are you doing?"

"Math is a good thing to be doing. Is it your homework?"

He shrugged. "I didn't get it done in class, so Mike told me to come out here and work on it for a little while. Then he would help me go over it."

"That sounds like a plan. Are you getting it okay?

Do you need my help?"

"No, I got it. It's easy."

"Then why did you not get it finished in class?"

"I was looking at Missy Briggs."

"And why were you looking at this young lady?"

"She's pretty. And she kept smiling at me."

Jesse hid a smile. "She did, did she? Well, maybe you should save staring at Missy until lunchtime or recess time. What do you think?"

The little fella sighed and studied his pencil for a minute before looking back up at him. "I can try. But her smile is mighty powerful."

Jesse's mind instantly filled with Caroline's sassy smile. "Yeah, I know what you mean. But at least try hard to get your work done at school. Then when you're home, you can get out there and hang out with the guys instead of sitting here working."

"I'll try."

He squeezed the kid's shoulder and then headed to the door. Gladys opened it before he reached it.

"I thought I heard your voice. Come on in. We're in Mike's office. Robbie, are you almost finished? Mike will look over everything after we talk to Jesse, okay, sugar?"

Robbie beamed at her. "I'll be finished. I promise."

The kid had a broad little face with big eyes and the glasses made them even bigger. Like him, Robbie had come to the ranch early and unless something miraculous happened, he would be here for the duration of his youth. He had been very sickly, and he'd nearly died before Mike and Gladys got him. Some of his organs had been affected and his health issues were going to be lifelong. It was a lot for a couple who wanted to adopt a child to commit to. These were many of the types of children who came through the ranch.

Jesse's determination rushed to the forefront of everything on his mind. This little kid and the other guys here deserved this stable, happy life that the ranch provided for them.

He walked with Gladys into the house and they went into Mike's office. Mike stood at the window, watching some of the boys in the backyard playing with Shaggy, their Australian Shepherd. He turned when Jesse closed the door.

Jesse stood just inside the room and surveyed the two people who meant the world to him. The people who had given him everything. "Okay, so, I'm here asking you to back off of this marriage requirement. There is no stipulation that legally keeps me from becoming the overseer of this boys ranch. I know y'all want to see me married but I'm not planning on doing that until I'm ready. Talbert McCoy is behind this, isn't he?"

Gladys slid her gaze to her husband, and Mike got that I'm-about-to-give-you-some-advice look that Jesse was well aware of after all these years. He had not been an easy teenager to raise. He had had his moments, and he and Mike had clashed many times. But he was grateful for every time Mike had stepped in. He had to trust him now. Or at least let him speak.

"Sit down, Jesse. And I'll give it to you straight. We are worried about you."

Jesse sat down in the old hard-backed chair that had been in this office for as long as he could remember.

"I know you don't think anything is wrong, but you are planning to take over this place, and we want you to. We were hesitant to tell you the truth. We don't believe it would be healthy for you to take this responsibility on just your shoulders." He held up a hand. "I know that you are a strong and decisive man who has excellent judgment and wisdom. You love this community, this land, this ranch and these boys. We know all of this. If not, you would have gone somewhere else and become whatever you wanted. You've stuck around and been a great mentor to the many boys who have come through since you did.

"But, for your own sake, we believe that you need a helpmate, someone beside you. I couldn't have done this without my Gladys. And she couldn't have done it without me. We are a team. And these boys deserve a team. I don't know if you realize it but all those times you were stubborn and wild would have been harder if I didn't have Gladys. Who knows how you would have turned out if my advice had been all you got. Without Gladys's love and support, it could have all failed. She is the heart that drives this place. Especially when you were young. She gives these boys a soft place to land—even the older ones—and you know it.

"So, we made that stipulation. It's in the best interest of our boys, too. We're always thinking about them."

"We hated to do it to you." Gladys's face gentled. "But we love you so much, Jesse, and we want what is best for you. If you would just let go of these issues that are keeping you from committing to one of them. We aren't certain what they are, but we know that something has kept you from committing to a woman. And you've dated plenty. The right woman is out there. We truly believe she is right under your nose."

Caroline, it was obvious.

Everyone believed they were the right ones for

each other. And he didn't help stop that belief because when she was around, he usually pushed her buttons because he couldn't stop himself. So the town had ideas, but they didn't understand that it was more from frustrations than anything else. *Why would a man want to marry a woman who had everything she could ever want?*

He could never marry a woman he had nothing to offer her.

It was a broken record that kept playing in his head.

He focused. "That's what I needed to know. Is there something else? Talbert?"

They looked at each other. Gladys rubbed her hands together, which was a clear sign that something was worrying her.

"We...we've decided that we want to go ahead and retire earlier, sooner than a month if possible. If you can find someone—we know that Talbert has stipulated that Caroline marry you, so we thought you might want to help her out. We just can't bring ourselves to say you have to marry Caroline in order to buy the ranch, but well, we hoped you might come to that decision on your own. It would help her out and us out. And yourself."

Mike nodded. "I'm sorry, son, but this is what

we've decided on."

Jesse crossed his arms and gave them a sardonic gaze. "You two have really bought into Talbert's plan. I talked to Caroline already about what her granddaddy is doing to her, and y'all do understand that even if I can convince her to go through with this fiasco that we won't make it? This is wrong. You know I'll do whatever it takes to keep these boys together here on the ranch. And she'll do what she has to do to keep funding this ranch."

At least they had the decency to look ashamed.

Mike cleared his throat. "We know that you probably think we are terrible people. But we are doing it out of love, and Talbert is too. We've watched you two dancing around each other all these years. You're crazy about each other and you know it. But you have something between you that won't let you take that next step. So, we are doing this now, to give you a shot. We are going to put the same stipulations on you that Talbert has put on Caroline. You must stay married for three months and after that the place will still be yours, but you and she can part ways. But our stipulation is that you two work civilly around these boys. They don't need any high drama, so you two will behave around them. I'm trusting you to honor that."

Jesse's temper was about to blow his Stetson right

off his head. Heat like a Texas summer day in the middle of August swept through him. He didn't trust himself to speak at the moment and just held Mike's gaze. He had never, ever expected these two to try to force him into something like this. He loved this ranch, these boys, and them. And they were dangling it over him like this.

He stood. "I need some fresh air."

With that, he turned on his heels and headed to the door. Without a backward glance, he opened it and strode down the hardwood floors and out the front door.

Robbie was about to come inside. The little bitty fella looked up at Jesse. That little smile of his cut deep into his heart.

"Jesse, I got it done, and I'm hoping I get to go on the cattle drive with everybody the day after tomorrow. Mike told me if I didn't get it done, I wouldn't get to go. And this will be my first time."

Jesse took a knee so he would be at Robbie's level. "I'm proud of you, and I know Mike's going to be proud of you too. And you know when he tells you something, he's doing it because he loves you and he wants what's best for you. I'll see you on that cattle drive 'cause I'm going along too."

Robbie's smile grew wide, from ear to ear, and his

glasses slid back down his nose. "I can't wait. I never got to go before. They wouldn't let me go until I was in first grade, so I'm excited. And I was so scared I messed up. I won't let no girl's smile keep me from my work ever again. I want to do cattle drives, so I'll start paying attention."

Jesse tussled his hair. "You'll have time soon enough for thinking how pretty the little girl sitting next to you is. Right now, enjoy living out here, riding these horses and cattle drives. So, go in there and share your good news with Mike and Gladys. She might even give you another cookie for it."

Robbie startled him when he threw his arms around his neck. "I love you, Jesse. Thank you for all your advice. I want to be a sheriff one day, but I have to grow some. When I told the other boys that, they told me Stonewall don't need a sheriff the size of me."

"Well, son, you made my day. I can tell you that your size has nothing to do with being sheriff. It's your heart and your ability to make good decisions. And Mike and Gladys—and I hope me—can help you with that. You already have a good heart. I can see it. And if you grow up and you're still short, that doesn't mean a thing. I have a lot of good friends who are a lot shorter than me, and they are just as good or better lawmen than I am."

Or had been. Because he knew soon, he wasn't going to be a lawman any longer...he was going to be the father figure to this boy and all the others who came to this ranch.

Unless Caroline couldn't find it in her heart to give him three months.

* * *

Feeling frustrated and conflicted by Tuesday, on Friday morning Caroline yanked on her cowboy boots and left her jeans half tucked into them. She didn't care; this was her country girl-gotta-get-along outfit. She'd pulled on her T-shirt that said, *You talking to me...* Yeah, she was mad. She'd gone over everything she could think of the last few days, made calls, and to no avail. She'd fought off the need to storm over to her granddaddy's house and give him a piece of her mind. Wouldn't do any good anyway, she knew he'd gone into Houston for business meetings, so she'd just be ranting to an empty house.

Instead she stormed out of the house and to her car. She knew exactly where she was heading when she stomped the gas pedal after turning her BMW onto the blacktop road. By the time she was almost to the curve, she was doing far over the speed limit to safely make it, so she slowed and was just doing a bit over the speed limit when she drove around the bend in the road, she was disappointed to see that he wasn't there.

Determined to find him, she drove on into town and spotted his SUV parked in front of Dixie's Diner. Stonewall was a small, spread out little town and Dixie's was in a row of older buildings that had been sitting on a side street for years. It was a favorite of the locals despite its faded and weary exterior. Her uncle JD had loved this place and taken his last breath inside eating Dixie's famous pecan pie. She hadn't been inside since the funeral.

Feeling jittery and anxious, she slowed her red sports car just as Jesse James came out onto the sidewalk. Adrenaline shot through her and she whipped into the slot beside his SUV.

Driven by the need to talk to him, she was out of the car almost before she'd rammed the shifter into park. She left the door open, yanked her T-shirt down over her jean's waistband, and barreled toward him. His dark expression told her his frame of mind was as bad as hers.

She stopped at the end of her car's hood and flung her arms open wide. "I'm so mad I could spit nails. The more I've thought about it, the madder I've gotten. This is wrong."

His brow crinkled appealingly. "Now, calm down, Caroline. I know exactly how you feel." He stuffed his hands on his hips.

She struggled to ignore what an appealing picture he made with those wide shoulders, slim hips, and uniform. And that face… Just looking at him calmed her a bit, but she wasn't going to admit that to him.

Instead she gave him a pointed stare. "Don't tell me to calm down, Jesse James. This is my life we're talking about." She stomped up onto the sidewalk and poked him in the chest. "Your life too. Doesn't that make you mad?"

"Yep." He jerked his head toward the windows, and she looked to see what he was trying to turn her attention toward. Several of the local ladies sat in a front booth having their weekly coffee and gossip session.

The swinging door of the diner opened and Amos and Martha, who owned the Flower Spot, a local flower farm and nursery came out onto the sidewalk.

Amos grinned a big toothy smile. "You two remind me of me and my Martha, here. We shot some fireworks off ourselves when we were courtin'." He winked at Caroline. "Martha was always trying to play hard-to-get too."

Martha smiled shyly. "He's right. But I finally

gave in to what my heart really wanted. And it's been forty-five years of fun living life with this man. You should just give in, Caroline. You know you want too."

"Everybody knows it," Amos declared. "I got twenty dollars in the pot down at the feed store on when the wedding date will be. My dates are pretty soon so you need to hurry it up if you know what I mean."

Caroline's mouth fell wide open. "Mr. Amos, you did not bet money on my marrying Jesse. Tell me you are just teasing me." She shot a glare at Jesse who was saying nothing. He had a half amused, half alarmed look on his face. She gave him an exasperated smirk and then bounced her glare back at Amos.

He looked like she'd just said something stupid. "Of course, I did. There's a bunch of us in the pot. Somebody is going to win three hundred dollars when you two finally tie the knot."

Martha placed her hand on her husband's arm and smiled at Caroline as if taking pity on her. "Come on, honey, let's let them get back to their…conversation."

"We'll do that," he said, grinning. "Y'all look like you might need to do a little kissing and making up. Get this wedding going if you know what I mean." He winked at them and then walked away with his wife.

"Well that was interesting," Jesse said, finally as

the couple walked down the sidewalk to their truck.

Caroline inhaled deeply, very deeply before she said anything. She was now in control and well aware of the many snooping eyes still watching them from inside. "Can we take this conversation around to the side of the building please," she said, and walked past him before he had even answered.

"Yes, ma'am, I believe that might be a safer way to have a private conversation."

"If you had been in your usual morning coffee drinking spot then we would be having this conversation on the side of a fairly deserted country road. What are you doing here anyway?"

"I came by for my normal breakfast sandwich. It's been a long morning and you're out far earlier than normal. I'm assuming you didn't sleep much?"

She spun once she stepped off the end of the sidewalk onto the side of the building, away from prying eyes. "You are right, I haven't slept since the whole fiasco started. So what did you find out about your situation? Is it like we thought? Are Mike and Gladys in cahoots with Granddaddy?"

"Cahoots, perfect word, they're scheming alright. And yes, your granddaddy got to them. But, like him, they believe they are acting in my best interest, and the boys' and in yours." He held up his hands when she started to protest. "I know, I know—they've all meddled too far where you and I are concerned. But Caroline, this is bigger than you and me. This is about the boys ranch. Yes, you and I are being manipulated in the worst ways and we don't like it at all. They are exploiting us because they know those boys our weakness. We can come out of this okay, you and me. But those boys—they need us."

Could he really be thinking what she was thinking?

"They need us more than we need to rebel."

Anger eased for a moment. "Yes. They do. And that's what makes me even more angry. That they would use these innocent boys to get to us."

He took his hat off and held her gaze. "I hear you loud and clear, heiress. I'm going to put it to you like this. I need you to marry me."

Her mouth went dry and her heart stumbled on his words.

"If you give me three months of your life, we'll keep the boys safe, make Mike and Gladys happy, and your grandfather, and at the end of three months, we walk away. And we'll both get what we want. I've got the same rules that you do. At the end of that time, I retain the ranch and you get your inheritance and the ability to continue to be a benefactor to the ranch. If you so choose. The only thing that will change is our marriage status." He inhaled. "That's it. To make it look more real to the town, we could get engaged for a couple of weeks…I could be your fiancé."

She recovered from the initial jolt of hearing him ask her to marry him. What was wrong with her? "My *fake* fiancé you mean," she added pointedly, needing for some reason to point out that this wouldn't be real. Nothing about it would be real except their signatures on the documentation. Just as real as the signatures on the divorce papers.

"Right, *fake* but real to everyone on the outside and on the paperwork."

Her stomach rolled. Oh, she felt so nauseous. She'd planned to lay it out there like this to him, but he beat her to it. It was shocking in so many ways.

Would a two-week engagement and a fake fiancé change anything? It would only add time to the end when they'd get the divorce and walk away free of each other and of her granddaddy.

She was going to have to marry him and then pretend that she didn't care.

Pretend that she could live without him.

Oh, she could live without him, she'd gotten used to the fact that he was never going to be hers. But being forced to marry him, live with him and then give it up…might be more than she could handle.

It was mean—mean of her granddaddy to do this. And wrong.

But she was not a quitter, nor could she turn her back on the kids who needed her. She nodded and blew out a breath. "Know, though, that at the end of three months, I'm going to walk away and set you free, but I'll always keep my commitment to those boys. After we split up, I'm going to move. I think I'm going to move to New York. My art has a better chance there and by then, I'll have cut all ties with Granddaddy. I can support the ranch from anywhere, so you won't have to worry about that."

His expression darkened and his gaze dug into her. She made her expression as unreadable as she could. Closed her heart tight.

"I don't think your granddaddy was wanting that."

"Right now, I don't care what he wants. This is his fault."

"So be it. When do you want to do this? Everyone in town is going to think it's real, just like with your brothers and cousins. It's a perfect storm. The engagement will—"

"Will only extend the inevitable." She raked a hand through her hair, her thoughts whirling like a tornado. "Okay, here's the deal Denton and Blaze ran off and did the deed on their own terms. I can have Beck or one of his pilots here within the hour. I don't want to extend this ruse or stand up there with you while everyone is so excited. I can't do it. And I refuse to give Granddaddy the satisfaction. They're all going to be so happy—you know I'm right. They are going to believe all this time they were right, and we were so in *love* with each other." She used her most exaggerated Texas drawl laced with sarcasm.

He smiled regretfully and that made tingles race through her. She wanted to stomp them with her boots. She might as well get used to those tingles because if she had to be around him day and night, then she was going to be a tingling sensation. It was ridiculous.

"I get where you are coming from. And on this, my thinking is that we should let everyone be involved. But I'm going to go along with you. We'll fly to Vegas or just go down to the city office. I can get it done. Whichever you want. And then we'll have a reception out at the ranch. The boys are going to be excited. I've been thinking about it—they're going to go through a transition when Mike and Gladys tell them what's happening. They respect me and even love me—most of them—but they think the world of Mike and Gladys and are going to be hurt when they find out they're leaving. We're going to have to be there for them and on our game to reassure them. Are you ready for that?"

Ready or not. "I'm ready."

"We have to make it good for them. We can't have any drama in front of them. They need to feel safe and loved, so when you get mad at me, when you want to twist my head off, we'll go out in the pasture somewhere and you can let me have it. I know you're going to be in as much strain as I am, or more."

He was amazing. She wondered whether he knew just how amazing he was.

"I hear you. And Jesse, I may not be happy about this, but I can do it. Although I have a feeling we are going to have to make a lot of trips out to that pasture."

CHAPTER SIX

Beck arrived within the hour, just like Caroline had said. He was waiting for them at the back of the McCoy Stonewall Jelly Farm and Winery. Jesse had called in and had his lead deputy take over for him for the next two days. Todd and Ginny met them there. Both of them looked amused by the situation.

Ginny hurried over to them with a big grin. "I knew you two would make this decision. I haven't been here long but I know you both care about the boys ranch. And I have high hopes love could blossom between the two of you. Hey, miracles do happen—Todd and I are examples of that. You've taken the bull by the horn and done this your way, even if that doesn't happen. We'll take care of your vehicles and keep your secret while you're gone. Won't we, Todd?"

Todd grinned. "Yes, ma'am, we will." He winked

at his wife and she winked back at him.

"You two are having entirely too much fun at our expense," Caroline said, arms crossed and her fingers tapping her biceps. "We are doing this under duress. I don't want to marry him but am doing it for the boys ranch. I am the last person he wants to marry." She glared at him defiantly.

He couldn't deny it. He didn't need anyone thinking he really wanted to marry her. "We're going to get through this." He gave her a frank, open look.

"You're right," she conceded. "I don't need to needle you to death. At the end of three months, all will return to normal."

Beck walked down the steps of the Learjet and knocked his hat back off his forehead. "You two are giving in, too? None of y'all are making it easy on me. But I can't judge you. Where do you want to go?"

"We're heading to Vegas for a quick trip. You can just wait on us. We won't be there long. We'll get the taxi driver to wait."

"You aren't going to use a car service? I can call one on the way."

The impact of that single sentence slammed into Jesse. Yeah, he was a taxi kind of guy, while the McCoys were car service/limousine kind of people. Before he could say anything, Caroline spoke first.

"Taxi. I'm not letting any car service alert Granddaddy to me eloping to Vegas. Or some tabloid. We're going in under the radar, I hope, as long as you don't make any unnecessary phone calls to limo services."

Beck's lip quirked. "Gotcha. Good thinking."

"I'm going to let Granddaddy figure it out on his own."

"Thanks for covering for us," she said to Ginny and Todd. "We'll owe you."

Todd waved her off. "You don't owe us anything. We've been through it and who knows, maybe you'll find a happily-ever-after."

"Ha," Caroline barked then strode toward the plane. "Come on, people. Time's a-wasting. Let's get this over with."

Jesse looked at the other three. "I don't know if she's really going to make it through this and keep her temper down."

Beck pulled his eyes away from his sister striding up the steps and disappearing inside the jet. "She will. It's the grudge that Granddaddy will have to deal with afterward. She'll be okay."

Jesse sighed tiredly, because he knew that was true. Caroline had a long memory; he knew it first-hand. She'd never let him forget kissing her. Or the fact that he wouldn't marry her, for real, because of her money.

* * *

The flight didn't take long. They grabbed a taxi and went to the first chapel they saw. He felt bad about it being so impersonal, but she wouldn't have it any other way. And it was for the best.

The wedding was short and to the point. Then Preacher Elvis told him to kiss his bride. He'd looked at her and his gut had knotted and every molecule in his body had surged forward in anticipation for that kiss. Caroline's eyes widened and her breath was shallow as he leaned in and pressed his lips to hers.

The world swam around them as her soft lips met his. She gave a small gasp then sank against him as his arms tightened around her in a possessive response that shook him to his core.

Short seconds passed that he wished could go on for a lifetime…as everything in his world was perfect for the time being as there were no barriers keeping them apart. It was just the two of them lost in the feel of each other as the frustrations that constantly played between them were given free rein to enjoy the passion that he as well as she, knew was always there between them. He deepened the kiss, wanting as much from that moment as he was allowed. Lost in the seconds ticking away before reality slammed full force into them.

In that instant Caroline yanked back, her dazed eyes took him in and melted his heart. Then they narrowed, shuttered and the heat that had melded them together got a cold dousing of reality. Her expression went stoic.

"Well, I guess that's that," she said flippantly. "I'm Mrs. Jesse James. I kind of feel like an outlaw."

His namesake. "Yeah, me too. Let's get out of here."

She nodded, then together they left the building. "Are you hungry?" he asked when they reached the sidewalk.

She wouldn't look at him he noticed and wondered if she felt as off-center as he did. That kiss had gotten out of hand. He should have been the one to stop it, but he hadn't been able to make himself do it.

"No. I want to get on the plane and get back. We have things to figure out, play by their rules for now but only for now." The anger that had been there before the kiss returned.

He glanced toward the sky filled with the tops of casinos and wondered whether they were really going to make it through this. He hated seeing her so angry.

He'd stewed about it the whole plane ride to Vegas too. She didn't deserve this. She deserved so much more. But he wasn't going to reach out to her in comfort like he longed to do and now even more. That kiss had just made his life harder than it was already going to be...it had upped the stakes, and made keeping his distance all the more important.

Wiping any emotion from his voice, he waved a hand toward the waiting taxi. "Then, your chariot awaits."

She was Caroline McCoy, his wife.

He just had to make sure she didn't turn into his bride. The way to do that was to keep all of his wants, desires, needs, and hopes to himself. She need not find out that he was going to have a really, really hard time keeping his hands off her.

* * *

She was married.

She was married to Jesse James.

Still reeling from what she'd done, Caroline stood in her bedroom with the double doors of her closet open wide. She stared at the clothes in her closet. It was actually so full there was no way she could pack it all and take it to Jesse's.

"How big is the closet at your place?" she called out to him. He was somewhere out in the living room of the pool house.

"Not big," he called. "Looks like you have a problem, heiress." He had come to the door of her room and leaned a broad shoulder against the doorframe as he studied her room with a casual glance. "I'm not familiar with too many pool houses, but that closet you're standing in is bigger than my bedroom. My house is an old farmhouse. They didn't make rooms very big, much less closets. Looks like you're going to have a problem."

She grimaced.

He hitched a brow. "I feel your pain. But I have confidence you can adapt." He smiled for the first time all day.

Her heart did a jig at that smile. "You do have two bedrooms, right?"

"I do have two bedrooms and even if I didn't, I'd sleep on the couch. You do not have to worry about that."

He said the words as if he didn't care, but she'd felt as much emotion from him in that kiss they'd shared in front of Preacher Elvis as she'd felt herself.

They were both going to be fighting temptation with every bone in their bodies.

She was Caroline James, his wife.

"But, once we move into the ranch house, we'll be sharing one room. And there's no getting around that."

She swallowed hard. Her stomach feeling bottomless at the dilemma they faced.

They'd started off that morning on a serious, depressing note and now, as the sun was going down, it was just as depressing. Shaking herself out of it, she grabbed her suitcase and rolled it from the closet.

He watched with interest and irritation slapped at her.

She straightened and glared at him. "This isn't funny. But we will figure it out. You'll stay on your side and I'll stay on mine. We're adults." She started to lift the large suitcase to her bed but he crossed the room in three long strides and grabbed the handle, his fingers sliding around hers, sending tingles of awareness racing up her arm and straight to her heart.

"Let me."

"It doesn't weigh much. Yet." She batted her lashes at him and told herself to let go of the handle and let him have it. They stared at each other. Her heart started tapping an SOS, and feeling breathless, she released the handle. "Knock yourself out."

His crooked grin sent fireworks shooting through her and setting her good sense wobbly.

"I'll do that." He hefted the oversized suitcase to the bed. "And I'll carry it out when you fill it up."

"Thanks." She proceeded to pull clothes from their hangers and grab them from her dresser. She packed all casual wear and, as an afterthought, added a few casual dresses and a pair of glittery sandals to the batch, along with a pair of running shoes.

She entered her bathroom, packed her makeup and shampoo into a bag, and carried that to the suitcase. She sighed and looked at Jesse, who stood calmly beside the bed, waiting. "I guess that's it. If I need anything else, I'll come get it. Now, let's go check out this new tiny closet I'm going to use for a short while."

"Let's do it. If you need more room, you can use my closet too. I'm actually impressed with your choices."

She closed the suitcase and zipped it up. "There you go. Take it away, cowboy."

He lifted it from the bed and carried it out into the living room to the front door. She watched him swagger away. She was really and truly doing this.

Every instinct she had told her to slam the door after him and lock it. This was a very bad idea.

But when he reached the door, he turned and looked back at her. "You coming, *heiress*?"

This was it, do or die. Run or hide. "I'm right

behind you, *cowboy.*"

He nodded and walked outside.

Trepidation filled her. This was her taking charge of a bad situation. This was her about to take the next step that would set her on a new course for her life. One that would ultimately lead her away from the home that she'd always known, the family she'd always loved and the man who was, a true thorn in her side but whom she could never have.

Taking a deep breath, she walked to the door, went outside and pulled the door shut behind her. She could do this.

She would do this.

CHAPTER SEVEN

Since she'd driven out to his house and left her car
there before they'd caught the plane to Vegas she
was riding with him now back to his house. They
didn't talk a lot on the way and Jesse was concerned.
Caroline had held up well but he knew she had to be
feeling a lot of emotions. She was shaking that right
leg of hers like she did when she was really uptight
about something. She was stewing over the whole
situation and she'd made it clear that she couldn't wait
to *not* be married to him.

Yeah, she'd made it abundantly clear over and
over again.

He glanced at her. "The boys have a trail ride
tomorrow, it's a teacher workday so they have the day
off and I've committed to taking them. Do you want to
come?" He looked back at the road but out of the

corner of his eye, he saw her head jerk toward him.

"Yes. That would be great. I need something to take my mind off all of this. And we need something to help us adjust to our new normal for now. Any idea how long before we take over?"

He kept his eyes on the road. "Not sure, but now that we're married, I have a feeling it won't be long."

"All right, then, let's do this. I'll go on the cattle drive and we'll see how it all unfolds. A trail ride will take my mind off of things. I haven't been on one in forever and it sounds fun. Just what I need."

He liked hearing her be positive. That was Caroline, always encouraging and also a take-charge kind of person. He never doubted that she would find a way to get through this. "I think the boys will love having you along. They are crazy about you."

"And I am crazy about them. That is the one bright spot in all of this. I'll at least get to spend time with them."

He was well aware of the fact that she said nothing about being excited about spending time with him. He pulled into his drive and parked the truck. He was aware that his house didn't even begin to compare to her pool house. He shrugged it off. Despite the fact that he had a problem with all of her money, he didn't particularly think about money very much. It got people what they needed and people who had an abundance could help places they loved, such as the boys ranch. He himself could live on little. As long as he had a patch of green around him, he was okay.

"Come on in and I'll show you where you're going to sleep. Then you can do whatever you want to do. I know this isn't the best, but we can make it work. We'll be at the ranch as soon as we find out their plans. I don't know about you but I'm kind of beat."

"Me too. And this will work. We'll get something to eat then call it a night."

It hit him that he hadn't thought about food since their snack on the plane. "Yeah, I have some sandwich meat and some bread. I didn't get to the store yet this week."

She squinted at him. A smile twitched at her lips. "You're going to feed me a sandwich on my wedding night? That's about right." She left the words hanging between them as she slid from the truck and closed her door.

He scowled, watching her. Then he got out of the truck and shut his door with a bit more force than necessary before he reached for her big bag. She'd been teasing with that remark, but it had highlighted the fact that this had been a long, hard day and all he had to offer was a stinking sandwich. What a guy.

"You really did pack this thing. Feels like a ton of bricks in here."

"If you had to pack your worldly possessions as fast as I did, you would probably pack a toothbrush and a clean pair of jeans and underwear and be done. I packed a bunch of jeans, so don't give me a hard time."

He laughed. "Point taken."

At the door, she paused while he pushed it wide.

"After you."

She slapped a hand to her cocked hip and hit him with mischievous eyes. "Aren't you going to carry me over the threshold, *darlin*'?"

Awareness raced through him. He fought the urge to lean forward and kiss her and startle the boots off her. "Oh, I would if you really want me to."

Heat flashed between them. He couldn't look away if he'd wanted to. This had always been their back and forth; they'd both felt the heat, the attraction, but both knew there was no future for them. It was something they couldn't help. Now it was dangerous.

"That's okay." She raked her gaze down him. "No touching allowed."

With that, she walked past him, through the living room and stopped at the dining table. He followed her in, acutely aware of how small and under decorated his home was. She surveyed the place. It was small but clean. It might lack dressing up but it had been remodeled at one point so at least the kitchen had fairly new appliances and the bathroom, the one and only bathroom had a new shower in it. That was a good thing. The bad thing—the only access to the bathroom was through his bedroom. The place had two bedrooms, both opened into the living room but the bathroom situation could be a problem.

"I can put you in my room since that is where the bathroom is, or you can use the spare room and use the bathroom whenever you need to. The laundry room is closer to the spare bedroom. It's up to you."

She considered that, looking from one door to the other. He saw her throat move as she swallowed hard.

"I'll take the guest room."

"If you're sure."

She walked to his doorway and looked inside at his rumpled bed. He always made his bed, but this morning he'd been distracted and had only been thinking about stopping her and telling her about the boys ranch. Now, he cringed at her seeing his disarray.

"I do make my bed. Just so you know."

"I'm not judging. I'm still taking the guest room."

"As you wish. Bathroom is yours anytime you need it."

"Good. Now let's get to making those sandwiches, then I'm taking a shower and going to bed. We have a cattle drive in the morning."

"Yeah, you're right. Five a.m. comes early." He walked over to the counter, pulled the bread out and set it on the counter. Very aware of her watching him, he walked to the refrigerator and pulled open the door. It was a sorry situation in there. He had a nearly empty bottle of mayonnaise—the real kind, not that sweetened stuff. And there was a nearly empty container of ham and a bottle of chocolate milk. This was pitiful.

"That's pitiful." She looked over his shoulder and echoed his thoughts.

He looked at her across his shoulder. Their faces were close. She could have leaned her head on his shoulder. "You want to go get something to eat?" He managed to sound normal despite feeling the strain of her closeness and the feel of her hand on his upper arm.

"Oh, no. I can live. Here, hand me that and I'll make them."

He reached for the mayonnaise and handed it to her. Their fingers touched and more heat raced through him. When he handed her the ham, he made sure they didn't touch. She moved to the counter and he went the opposite way to the coatrack. He removed his hat and hung it on a peg. Then he went to the sink and rolled his shirt sleeves up while she washed her hands. When she moved out of his way, he grabbed the soap and washed. He was drying his hands and watching her when it hit him. *Caroline McCoy was really in his kitchen. Strike that.* He amended the thought. *Caroline* James *was in his kitchen.*

The bad part about it was that if it wasn't for her money, he liked the sound of that a lot.

* * *

Mike had called and told Jesse they should bring a suitcase when they came to the ranch for the trailride because he and Gladys were planning to leave that day for Montana. It had been a surprise that they were turning over the boys to them so quickly, but they loaded up some things and headed over. The boys were excited when they arrived. Their faces exploded with joy when they realized that Caroline was riding too. She felt a huge twist of gratefulness for that. After last night, going to bed straight after their sandwiches, she had lain in that bed knowing that Jesse was just across the small house and it had just about driven her crazy. They were a sorry, sad sight.

That morning, she had been startled out of sleep by a sound in the kitchen. She had gotten up and walked outside her room to find him making coffee. She had worn yoga pants and a T-shirt that was way oversized to bed and hadn't even worried about her tousled hair. All she was thinking about was that she was so groggy and needed that cup of coffee. But the moment she saw him standing there, barefoot, with his jeans hanging low and a white T-shirt stretched across his torso and his hair wet from the shower, her heart had pretty much fallen to her feet and bounced a few times, and she had lost her breath.

She was pathetic, standing there with her mouth open.

"Coffee." He had handed her a cup.

"Thanks," she muttered as their fingers brushed, and then she'd escaped to the shower.

They had barely spoken to each other on the drive out. But she had felt his gaze several times. Now, seeing little Robbie come running toward her and the other boys grinning from ear to ear, her heart swelled and she was glad she was here. Seeing them helped her focus on what her real mission was. It had nothing to do with Jesse; it had everything to do with saving her inheritance so she could help these boys when she wanted and how she wanted.

Robbie flung his arms around her. "Miss Caroline! Miss Caroline, you are here! This is my first cattle drive. Are you going too?" He looked up at her with big ole eyes, his little glasses haywire on his face after he had hugged her so hard, knocking them crazy.

She reached down and straightened his glasses, then rubbed the top of his head. "Yes, I am. I'm excited, too. I haven't been on a cattle drive in a long time, so we'll have to help each other out. How does that sound?"

His little eyes were dazzling. "That sounds like the best surprise ever." He looked at Jesse as he came around the corner of the truck. "Jesse, you didn't tell me Miss Caroline was coming. This is going to be fun."

Jesse winked at the boy. "I had to keep some surprises from you. It's a special day. So anyway, let's all get up there and get our horses ready. You got yours picked out?"

"Oh yeah, I'm riding Doodle."

"Doodle?" Caroline chuckled. "Who named him that?"

"I don't know. Somebody donated him to us little kids. So that's where I've been reg…regulated. Did I say that right?" She met Jesse's laughing eyes and looked back at

Robbie. "I think you meant relegated to riding him."

"Yes, that's it. Mike said Doodle was the best horse for me until I can get my skills up better. Because I had an accident on a horse and fell off. Mike said I was lucky I didn't break my neck. I don't want to break my neck. And I like riding Doodle. I wish he had a better name, though."

"I think it's a cute name. And anyway, we can't all have great names like Jesse James. You know what I mean?"

"Yeah, old Jesse's got a famous name, doesn't he? He's all dangerous."

Jesse looked at them. "I'm not dangerous. I don't know what my parents were thinking when they gave me that name. I took a lot of teasing growing up with that name."

"But you grew up to be a lawman instead of an outlaw. And that's good, right?"

Jesse gave the little boy a stern look. "Yes, Robbie, that's the best. Now let's quit talking about being an outlaw and all that stuff. Let's go get our horses. I'm anxious for today to start. Where's Mike and Gladys—do you know?"

Tony, one of the older boys, pointed toward the house. "They're inside. I don't think they're going. They said we were supposed to wait for y'all."

"Y'all go get the horses ready. We'll go see Mike and Gladys."

The boys headed toward the stable.

Jesse looked at Caroline. "Come on, let's go see them. I told them on the phone we were married. I thought I might as well get it out in the open before we got here."

They went to the house and he tapped on the back door.

Gladys opened the screen. She smiled widely. "Come in, come in." Soon as they were inside, she hugged Caroline. "We are so excited about you two getting married. We didn't expect it quite so soon but we've been making plans." She stepped back, excitement just radiating off her.

Caroline actually hadn't seen the old woman look quite this excited ever before. She wasn't sure what to say to her excitement. "Thank you for forcing us to get married" didn't exactly seem appropriate. She decided to be direct but not mean, that wouldn't do anyone any good. "Thank you, Gladys. But you do know we had to do this under force. But, I'm glad it's helping you and Mike. You deserve to retire."

Gladys had the grace to look a bit ashamed. "Yes, well, you're right and I'm just praying it all works out."

Mike came into the room. He was dressed in his usual jeans and button-up shirt. He smiled at her. "Congratulations, you two. As I said on the phone, we've decided that since y'all already married that we would go ahead and get out of y'alls way. We're going to go out there in a minute, and we're going to tell the boys we're taking a little vacation. We don't have to tell them just yet that we're not coming back. We'll ease them into that. Y'all can move in here when y'all get back, and we'll head on out. How's that sound?"

Jesse stepped up beside her. "Y'all go relax somewhere and we'll take care of them. Don't worry about anything. And when you're ready, we'll tell the boys everything."

Mike slipped his arm around Gladys's shoulders. "Thank you. It's a big relief knowing the boys are in good hands."

Gladys smiled again. "I think it sounds wonderful. It will give me and Mike time to adjust to not being here with them all the time."

Caroline did not hear any mention of her and Jesse needing to ease into this. No one seemed to worry about them. But that was okay; the sooner they could get this started, the sooner it could be over.

"That sounds like the perfect plan for everybody." She was quite proud of herself for saying that without too much ire. She met Jesse's gaze and he gave her a slight nod. She knew he had realized that it had taken a lot for her to keep her mouth shut.

"Okay, then, let's do this." He opened the door wide and they all trailed one another out onto the front porch.

The boys came out of the stable with the horses. At this time, there were only five boys at the ranch. They could hold ten but he was grateful at the moment that there were only five.

Mike called them over and when they all gathered round, Mike told them the news. "Fellas, we waited until this morning to let you know that me and Miss Gladys are going to take a little vacation. We're going to go see my sister up in Montana for a couple weeks. And Jesse and Caroline are going to stay here and look out for you guys…well, I'll let them explain it all to you. We just wanted y'all to know that we love y'all, and we'll be thinking about y'all while we're gone. Y'all okay with all that?"

"Yes, sir," Tony said and the other boys echoed him. He was seventeen and everybody usually looked to him. He looked from one to the other then nodded. "We're good with that. Aren't we, boys? Y'all need some time off. Goodness, we know it ain't easy watching all us boys."

"Y'all deserve it," sixteen-year-old Greg added.

"Now, we have some news. Caroline and I got married yesterday, and we wanted to share that with y'all first before we shared it with anybody else."

Excitement erupted among the boys. All of them came forward, grinning. Tony held his hand up to Jesse and congratulated him like a grown man.

Caroline thought that was so cute, and she reminded herself that she was going to not have to think about the bigger boys as cute—they might not like that. But after they had taken hugs and congratulations and little Robbie had very nearly hugged her to death, her heart twisted in ways she had never known it could. And she realized that being out here with these boys and then leaving might be really hard. Might be harder than she realized. She had never been completely responsible for them; she had just been a person who handed them the money they needed and she would come out and help sometimes. All this hugging, really getting in there and helping them on a day-to-day basis…this might be harder than she ever even imagined.

* * *

After they had all loaded up and ridden out into the pasture for the first time since all this started, Jesse's tension eased. Riding on this ranch had always been a blessing to him. He scanned the horizon, knowing they still had several pastures to go through before they reached the cattle. The drive would get them back home so they'd be ready for trucks to pick up many of the calves that were for sale. It was not a huge cattle drive, but mostly for the boys to experience one and to have some fun. He remembered the first time he'd gotten to go on a cattle drive; he was probably as excited or more excited than Robbie.

Mike had probably been about his own age at that time and he had been awesome. Now as he surveyed the groups spread out, riding side by side across the land, he smiled at the thought that he was going to get to do this with them on a permanent basis.

It felt right. He looked over at Caroline, wondering how she was doing. She rode straight in the saddle and yet she looked relaxed. She'd pulled her curly hair into a ponytail, exposing her neck. She wore a red tank top and her golden skin glistened from a slight sheen of perspiration. It didn't take long in this Texas heat for everyone to perspire. But even sweat on Caroline was attractive; it made her skin glisten and look dewy in the sun. He tore his gaze away before she looked at him, not wanting her to catch him staring. His gut rumbled as he fought the thoughts from last night. They had parted early, her heading to her room and closing the door firmly between them. He had sat in the kitchen for a few minutes, finishing his ice tea and staring at that door. He still couldn't believe they were married. Finally, he had gotten up and gone to bed, only to lay staring up at the ceiling in the dark. His mind had been full and it had taken him a long time to shut down and go to sleep.

He'd been up early and making breakfast when she had stumbled out of the bedroom, looking mussed and beautiful. It had been almost all he coud do to not take her in his arms…which would have been a very bad idea. He had been thankful when she went to the shower and had closed the door behind her. Of course, then he had to think about her in the shower. Didn't matter if they were married. None of that mattered. Hands off was their rule.

At least last night they'd been in separate bedrooms. Tonight, they'd be moving into the ranch house. Because by the time they got back to the ranch house, Mike and Gladys were going to be gone. They had told them they'd moved their things out of the master bedroom, stored them in one of the now-empty rooms, and left the master bedroom for them. And so tonight his clear and present danger was going to be learning to sleep in the same room with her and not go crazy.

Pushing the thoughts out of his mind, he pointed on the horizon when he spotted several deer racing across the pastures. "We've got company up ahead."

Archie, ten years old and red-headed, grinned over at him. "I just like watching them fellas run. I saw a hog the other day, too. Mike showed me what they do to the ground and that's not pretty, so I'm not one to like a hog. You think we can go hog hunting one day?"

He had been raised hog hunting. In Texas, hogs could shred people's land. They were horribly destructive, and they multiplied at an unreal level. Hog hunting was almost a necessity.

"Well, we might think about that. I need to get y'all some more lessons about holding guns and treating them with respect, but yeah, we'll do that, Archie. Think you can handle that?"

"Yes, sir, I can."

"What about you, Kyle?" he asked Kyle, the eleven-year-old riding beside Archie.

"Yes, sir, I can do that. Mike says I'm really good with a .22. I got to shoot a skunk the other day that was acting crazy. We was afraid it might have rabies or something—you know how they get. It was weaving and it was losing hair. It was nasty looking."

"Well, that's a good thing. That's how we keep the land and the animals healthy. You did good—you weeded out a bad one. You're right—if they're losing hair like that and they're weaving around, it's not a good sign. Did he take it to the vet?"

Greg spoke up. "Yes, sir, he did. He didn't tell you? And, yes, sir, it did have rabies. So we've been watching them and if we see a skunk, we're supposed to pay close attention and stay away from them. But of course we're not going to go try to play with a skunk anyway."

Jesse laughed, but he planned to call Mike and ask him about that, and the vet too. "Yeah, I'm thinking that you guys are a little bit smarter than wanting to go play with a skunk…but you never know."

Tony called from where he was riding. "Well, we have to keep ole Robbie here away from them. He thinks they're cuddly."

"I do not! I ain't that dumb," Robbie snapped.

Tony grinned. "I'm just teasing, you little squirt. I know you're smarter than that. But you know we've had some city boys who have come here before and they might have wanted to play with them, so we have to make sure."

He knew they were talking about Alex. Alex had not played with skunks but he had come to the ranch last year and he just hadn't liked it. Hadn't liked anything about the ranch. He had let them all know it—he liked the city. Sadly, he had gotten into a lot of trouble. There had been nothing they could do to reach him. He didn't want to be in the country; he wanted to be in the city. He wanted to be somewhere where there were things he recognized—loud music and video games. Here at the ranch, that wasn't one of the things these boys liked. They enjoyed getting outside and he was thankful for it, but his heart had been heavy ever since Alex left. He had kept up with him, and though the kid had struggled he seemed to be doing better now.

He recognized that they couldn't always work out for a kid, but Jesse knew that he welcomed the challenge of helping all who came their way. They had a good group here who had adapted and loved what they did but it wouldn't always be so. He wondered whether Caroline had ever thought about that—it wouldn't always be easy.

They reached the gate. Tony rode up ahead and opened it for them, grinning as they all passed through. "Just one more gate, fellas, and we'll be there. Mike had me ride out yesterday and check up on them and there's a good-sized herd."

They would be traveling a slower route to the holding pens and would be traveling in one section along the river. It could be tricky there.

CHAPTER EIGHT

Caroline was enjoying herself, despite all the craziness. By the time they reached the cattle, she had relaxed. Her spirit was calmer and, for the first time since all of this started, she was having a good moment. She had not let Jesse catch her, but she had watched him from the corner of her eye several times. The man was in his element. Oh, he was a great lawman—always had been—but there was an edge to him, a restlessness. She had always seen it but here on the land, on the horses with the boys, it was easy to see he was meant for this.

And in her heart of hearts, she was glad for him. Glad she was able to do something to help him get his heart's desire. She put that out of her mind as she knew she wasn't going to get hers. But there was just something about being able to make him happy that was a good thing. Now, as she looked at the cattle grazing around her, she felt a little hum of challenge. It had been a long time since she'd ridden a horse and tried to keep cattle moving. Now cowboys would tell you it wasn't a big deal but for a person like her, who hadn't ridden in a while, it was going to be a challenge to see whether she could still stay in the saddle if one broke from the herd and she had to go after it. Or her cattle horse decided to dig its hooves in and block the runaway.

Hopefully, with the bigger boys, Jesse had some good help, and they could keep the herd under control. Robbie was barely comfortable in the saddle. Thankfully, Doodle seemed like a good, calm horse for him.

"Jesse, where do you want me? And are you going to take the back and what about Robbie?"

"I'm going to keep him with me, and we'll ride the back. You ride over on the right side. When we get to the river, stay away from it. And if a calf gets away—or any of them—we'll take care of it. Tony knows how to do it. So does Greg. And Archie and Kyle, from what Mike filled me in on, are decent riders. But I told them all that when we get to the river, they're all to stay to the side away from the river. If the cows want a drink, they can have one. We don't need anybody riding over there, especially when we get to that area where the river converges into that one rushing area. No riders need to take a trip down the Pedernales River today."

"You're not going to hear me complain. Although I have ridden the Pedernales River several times."

"In an inner tube. We're not inner tubing today and the river is up, so we don't want to be in there."

They looked at each other. They knew that they had both been down the Pedernales River together a time or two back when they were young, back before they realized they were going to grow up and have this problem between them. Once, they had an easy-going relationship—before the hormones kicked in and messed everything up.

She hitched a brow at him. "You never know…I may have an inner tube in my saddle bag back there."

"Well, I suggest you keep it in there because if you fall in accidentally, maybe you can pop it open and I won't have to come in after you."

"Ah, now that sounds promising. If I thought I could get you to come in the water and I could see you swim out there, I think it might be worth it."

"Don't be giving me a hard time. If I have to come in the water that means I won't be out here with the kids."

"Like you said, they can handle it. I think they're very capable."

He shook his head. "I know you're joking. At least, I hope you're joking."

"I'm joking. I've got my new boots on—I don't want to go in the water."

He looked down at her old worn boots. "Those aren't new. How long have you had those, anyway?"

"They might not be new but I wouldn't give them up for the world. They're the most comfortable pair of shoes I own and I've owned them since high school, when my feet quit growing. I didn't see any reason to get rid of them. They're my sassy boots."

"They're your bull stomping boots. Your I-don't-take-anything-from-anybody boots."

She almost laughed and her heart clenched a little bit. He knew her. "Yes, they are. They make me feel invincible."

He smiled. Reached out and, to her surprise, tugged a curl gently, sending a shiver down her. "You're invincible no matter what, Caroline." And then he rode off, hollering instructions to the boys.

She took a deep breath and reminded herself that she was invincible. Right now, she just didn't feel exactly that way. As she watched him ride away, thoughts about later tonight when she was going to have to sleep in the same room as him had her feeling even less invincible. Life was about to get interesting.

* * *

She had been enjoying the ride, watching the guys as they rode along beside the cattle. They were keeping them moving.

She'd been on a ranch all her life and had been thankful that her granddaddy had raised her that way, even though they had all that money that he had made and her daddy had made. And her uncle J.D. had done the same—they'd all been raised to work on the ranch. Of course, she hadn't completely appreciated it back then, and as she got older, she took up shopping and spas more than thinking about getting all sweaty with a bunch of cattle. But watching these boys brought back memories. Good memories. Jesse had worked cattle with them on the McCoy ranch. He and her brothers and cousins had all been friends; he'd come help them out sometimes, and they'd come help the boys ranch when needed. The boys ranch didn't have a big enough cattle operation that it made any money, but Mike believed, like her granddaddy did, that working cattle and riding horses gave a boy purpose and built a good man.

And it gave him something to do out in the beautiful sunshine. She thought there was something to that now because Jesse had gone through a stage of rebellion and had quickly come back to being a great guy. She tore her eyes away from him as a calf broke from the herd and ran her way. "Ya!" She waved her arm. "Haw," she yelled more forcibly.

The calf immediately turned and rejoined the herd.

She smiled, and a little bit of her confidence returned. She'd had her expensive heels on the day before and today she'd traded them in for her comfy boots. She decided that she might just keep them on for the duration of this three months married to Jesse.

It didn't take them long to travel to the river. They'd come in to get the cattle one direction but that wasn't the way they had to take them back. This way to the cattle pens on the opposite side of the ranch took longer and avoided the ravine that ran through certain sections of the ranch, which they wanted to avoid. It took longer to chase runaways out of there than was worth it and sometimes it took days to find some and they'd miss the sale. The river had its own challenges but only had one small stretch of high banks that could be a challenge. All the boys who'd lived on the ranch had always loved this ride, and no one had ever had trouble. If they got through that one spot and nobody fell into the river, they would be great. All the boys could swim—so could she—but accidents happened.

As they neared that stretch of land, she felt uptight. She told herself she'd been thinking about it too much and also because this was her first time fully responsible for the boys, she was just overreacting. The calf that had tested her several times on the ride did it again, not helping her jitters as they reached the narrow strip. Her horse was quick on its feet and hadn't let the calf get by all morning. But as she cut left to stop the calf, a rabbit raced out of a bush and into the herd's path. The calf that had been racing her way freaked out and several others did too, coming her way as the herd all reacted. Instantly, cattle went everywhere.

And Caroline's horse startled her. It reared up and then came down hard, jolting her before it started turning in circles and then bucking.

She held on as cattle raced everywhere. The boys yelled and she could hear Tony yelling directions. She heard Jesse yell for Robbie to hold on and knew something had happened with Robbie. She held on to the saddle horn as her horse just went berserk. She had never been on a rampaging horse. She heard Tony yell and saw him riding toward her, just as her horse bucked to the edge of the river. She knew she was going in; she just prayed that the horse didn't go in on top of her. Tony's terrified face was the last thing she saw as the horse reared backward and both of them plunged over the edge.

* * *

When chaos broke out, Jesse's horse had turned and run the opposite way. Jesse spun his horse and raced after them. He reached Robbie and got him off the horse—thankfully, safe. Tony's yelling had him spinning his horse in time to see Caroline's horse rear and fall off the edge of the riverbank backward.

Holding onto Robbie, he urged his horse into a gallop and raced back to help. His heart thundered and his stomach churned. He yelled fiercely for Tony to stay back. The kid had dismounted, and he knew he was going in after her. Jesse barked out orders for him to stay where he was. If Caroline had gone in and that horse landed on top of her, if her foot got tangled in a stirrup or her belt buckle on a saddle horn—it would not be good. Then again, if she fell loose and swam away, she had a chance, and he didn't need two in the water to try to save.

"I don't see her!" Tony was not happy, staring downstream as he reached him. "I don't see her! I don't see her!" he continued yelling.

Jesse's heart slammed against his chest as he scanned the water. He saw the horse's head but he didn't see her. He handed Robbie down. The kid was shaking, he was so distressed. "Tony, I need you to take Robbie. You're in charge. Keep the boys back—get them together. I don't care where the cattle go. You just get the boys together. I'll meet you downstream. None of you go into that water for any reason. I don't care what happens next—you keep the boys safe. You hear me?"

Tony got himself together. "Yes, sir. Go. I've got this."

With that assurance, Jesse slapped his horse on the rump and it bolted into a gallop. He rode as fast as his horse could carry him along the bank, scanning the water and praying that she would come up somewhere along the river's edge. When he spotted her head bobbing not too far from the frightened horse as it swam, trying to keep its own head up in the current, Jesse urged his horse faster. Her head went back under and he felt in his gut something wasn't right.

Riding hard, he passed the horse in the water and moved his horse to the bank and into the shallow water. He could see the other horse and beside it, he saw Caroline again. *She was still alive.* Keeping his eyes glued to her, he waded in the thigh-deep water. Then he dove into the water and fought hard against the current to reach her.

"My foot," she gasped.

He snagged her arm then lunged for the horse. Grabbing its saddle horn, he pulled her to it. Then, sucking in air, he went under and fought to pull her foot from her boot. It had gone through the stirrup and she would never have gotten it out herself. Knowing he was hurting her, he yanked hard and she was free. He came up as she lost her hold on the horse. He grabbed her, turned her on her back, and then stroked for shore. The river widened here and the current wasn't as strong. The horse found its way to the shallows ahead of him, and he was thankful when his feet touched bottom. Stumbling, he carried her out of the water and collapsed onto the muddy bank.

"Caroline." He said her name, looking into her pale face, and when she opened her eyes, he pulled her to him. "Thank God." *He'd almost lost her.*

He sucked in deep breaths, and she breathed hard against him. "Are you hurt anywhere other than your ankle? Did the horse hurt you when it fell on you?"

"I'm fine. My ankle is throbbing but…" She paused for breath. "The water was deep, so the horse didn't hit me. Thank you."

He looked down at her. Water dripped from her lashes; her hair was all across her face. He took one hand, the other still wrapped around her, and gently pushed the hair off her face. He took that moment to hold her tight. "I've never been so scared in all my life. I'm sorry. Caroline, I'm so sorry. I didn't foresee something that bad happening there."

"It's not your fault. Weird things happen."

"Yeah, but this is my first day watching these kids and you, and I let this happen. I could have lost you. We could have lost you." He covered up his words.

She let her gaze slide away from him. Saw the boys coming their way. He did too.

"I'm fine, Jesse. Don't scare these boys. You get me back to the house or you get me on a horse—I'm fine. We'll tend to my ankle after we get there. Just don't scare them."

"I won't. We'll get you home and we'll tend to that ankle. You sure you feel okay on the inside? You sure you didn't get too much water?"

"I got up out of the water enough that I'm fine. Now come on."

He was rambling. He nodded, took a deep breath, willed his knees to hold him and then stood. He was waiting for the boys when they reached them. All of them were pale with worry.

"How is she?" Their questions echoed.

"She's shaken and I am too. Y'all did good. Let's get Caroline back to the house. I need to look at her ankle and we'll take care of these cattle later."

Tony looked down the way where the cattle were far in the distance behind them, content and calm. "I can get them back. Me and Greg—we can do it." He stared at Tony hard. His gut told him to say no but he knew that was just fear for Caroline. His first major decision after his first major near-disaster. With a solemn nod, he gave Tony the okay. "You do it. But if they give you the least little bit of trouble, you let them go and take it slow."

Caroline patted his heart, he assumed in agreement with his decision.

"Yes, sir."

"Yes, sir." Greg joined in Tony's agreement.

Looking shaken, Robbie scrambled down from where he was riding behind Tony.

"I'll ride with Archie."

"Good idea. You three come with me." They all disagreed, except for Robbie.

"I don't need y'all to disagree with me right now. Sometimes you have to take instructions and not disagree. Right now, I don't need to be worrying about y'all out here while I'm worrying about Caroline's well-being. So, man up and let's go."

As if understanding that he had more than he wanted or needed on his plate, they agreed.

Tony handed him his reins to his horse that had been waiting patiently. He set Caroline in the saddle.

"I can ride," she protested.

He stuck his foot in the stirrup and loaded up behind her, drawing her close. "I don't need any lip from you either, Caroline. You'll ride with me." And to his surprise, she settled against him and said nothing more.

CHAPTER NINE

She hated feeling helpless.

Caroline rode drenched, on the horse, once again snuggled in Jesse's arms. Even the universe was conspiring against her.

His arms were securely around her as they rode together all the way back to the ranch. Her ankle throbbed but she was barely aware of it. She was more than aware of Jesse's hard chest against her back.

"You doing okay?" he asked.

"I'm fine, just worried about my ankle and not being able to do my part while at the ranch."

"Don't worry about that. We'll manage. Right now, we just need to get you home and to get some ice on it. I could care less about you helping around the ranch. That is nothing compared to what just happened and how close we came to losing you."

His concern was touching. She fought hard not to make too much of it. He would have been concerned like this for anyone. "It was scary but you got there."

His arms tightened around her and she closed her eyes and for just this ride home, she let herself sink into him and enjoy the moment. Grateful she was alive to enjoy it.

When the house finally came into view, she'd gotten her wits about her again.

"Thank goodness," she muttered. "Seemed like it's been forever to get here."

He chuckled. "You want out of my arms that bad?"

"Well, I have to tell you the truth, this saddle horn is killing me."

"So that's your story."

"That's my story and I'm sticking to it. But really, I'll be glad to get out of your arms, Sheriff."

"I hear you loud and clear."

They rode the rest of the way in silence. She wondered why she'd brought needling into the conversation. Self-preservation, she assumed.

When they reached the house, he dismounted and then reached for her.

"I can get down myself."

He looked exasperated. Then looked over at the

boys who had ridden ahead and were waiting for them. "Y'all take the horses and brush them down and let them cool off. Y'all did good today. What happened was not your fault. Sometimes weird accidents happen that change plans. You handled yourselves well."

He turned to her and then took her by the waist, ignoring her protest, and pulled her into his arms. "Not a word. I'm carrying you inside."

She sighed. The boys were watching and all she could do was smile and go along with the plan.

* * *

Jesse lowered Caroline into a chair and propped her ankle in another chair, pulling the chair a comfortable distance so she could bend her knee if she needed to. Her ankle was in terrible shape, swollen and bruised. *He* was in terrible shape after having had to hold her close for over an hour on the ride back.

He walked over and grabbed two bags of frozen peas from the freezer. Then he got a hand towel out of the drawer and returned to wrap her ankle in the towel, then placed one bag under her ankle and one on top.

"They form to your ankle better than ice. Is there anything I can get you? Would you rather be in the bedroom, on the bed?"

"No, this is good. I'm fine."

He shifted from foot to foot, uncertain. He was in new territory. Not of taking care of people but of taking care of Caroline. He wanted to do more for her but in the end, he just nodded and let it go.

"You sure you don't need some water, coffee, or tea? Gladys keeps tea in the refrigerator."

She studied him then smiled. "I'll take a glass of water and a cup of coffee."

At last, something to do. "Sounds good." Tension radiated between them just like it had on the ride to the ranch. Holding her in his arms had been a struggle. It had been too enjoyable.

It had left him wanting more.

He went to the refrigerator and pulled open the door. A pitcher of ice water and a pitcher of tea sat inside. He grabbed the water and filled two glasses. He carried one and set it on the table in front of her.

"Thank you." She took a sip. "I needed that more than I realized."

He studied her. Thoughts of holding her in his arms flashed into his mind. He'd had a longing in his heart that holding her could be an enjoyable time if he let it, but it wouldn't work and so it was rough, a torture that nagged at him. He could never be good enough for her. So he certainly didn't need to keep entertaining thoughts of her soft body next to his and her big eyes looking at him like he was all she could ever want or need. Nope, that was not the truth and he needed to remember that.

All the reasons he wasn't good enough for her rolled through his mind, lack of money being one. Lack of not being able to provide for her in a way she was used to.

That didn't stop him caring though. His fear for her broke back into his thoughts. How scared he'd been when he hadn't been able to see her in the water. His heart raced, thinking about it.

He spun and went to the coffeemaker. He grabbed a filter, then coffee, and finally filled the reservoir with water and started the coffee brewing.

"I'll go grab you a towel. What am I thinking? Then I'll give you a warm cup of coffee and I'll go grab our suitcases in and change. Then you can change after that ice is on your ankle a few more minutes."

"Sounds good." She gave him a smile. "Don't look so gloomy, Jesse. Surely the next three months can't be as wild as our first day."

"I'll go for that." He held his hand up and she slapped her hand against his in a high five. They stared at each other and that kinship that had always been between them early on returned for that moment. The friendship they'd shared long before their hormones had kicked in and come between them had been simple. A time when they'd raced through pastures after calves, or gone fishing on the bank of that very river.

"We're going to make it."

She nodded. "Yes, we are. Now, that towel."

He laughed. "Coming right up." He turned and headed for the laundry room, his spirits lifted. They would get through this.

* * *

By that evening, Caroline was dry and sitting on the couch in the living room. She was positioned on the end of the couch with her ankle propped on a pillow. She had six male nurses tending to her every need. This was something she had never anticipated, but they were all adorable, including their leader. Jesse had hovered until she'd finally told him he should go get their things at his place. He had put the boys in charge and done as she'd asked, and brought them to the ranch while she had been plied with coffee, tea, water, cookies, and all kinds of other offers that appeared without having to ask for it. She was touched and decided that this was going to certainly be an interesting ride over the next three months.

Finally, she looked at Tony. He was taking a moment to flip through a wildlife magazine. "Tony, what time do y'all normally go to bed?"

All the boys turned their attention to her.

"Do I have to tell you?"

She laughed. "Yes. I think it would be a good idea if we kept the same routines while Mike and Gladys are gone."

The boys looked at Tony, and he looked at them apologetically, then heaved a sigh. "They're in bed by nine. But we don't have to go to sleep. We just have to go to our rooms. Mike and Gladys are usually pretty worn out by then. Especially lately. I kind of figured since you and Jesse are younger that maybe y'all wouldn't be so tuckered out by nine. That maybe we could squeeze in another hour down here before going to our rooms. We're all pretty good size now—older, I mean—except for Robbie there. He's small in size and age." He grinned, obviously unable to resist teasing the little boy.

Robbie scowled. "If y'all can stay up till ten, I can too. I ain't that little."

Caroline understood their need to stay up. Especially Greg and Tony. Nine was early. "I tell you what. Tonight, because with the day we've had and the ankle ordeal, I am tired, so let's go with Mike and Gladys's rules, and then that way we can wake up in the morning and evaluate how everyone is doing. Then Jesse and I will make some decisions together. We'll see what he thinks."

To her relief, they all nodded in agreement. *How had she been so lucky to get these boys who were so amicable?* She remembered when Jesse had first come to the ranch. She'd been young and they hadn't hung out then. But she remembered hearing that he had begun testing his will against Mike's pretty early. It was a natural thing, nothing alarming. And it wasn't because he was a foster kid; it was because he'd been abandoned by his parents. Her brothers had gone through it and she had, too, in some ways, rebelling after their parents had died. As she thought about her unique and tragic past, it gave her some insight into what these kids coming here to the ranch were going through. It was sobering to know that she could take such a horrible circumstance—a terrible part of her past—and maybe use it for good when trying to understand what boys at the ranch could be going through. It was a very odd feeling.

But, if she'd had to go through something so terrible and she'd learned from it, then it would be a way of honoring her mom and dad by being able to use her past to help others through their grief, whatever it might have come from. Her heart swelled at the idea.

This was something she hadn't expected. Her throat clogged as she looked at them. "You boys are awesome. Have I told you that today?"

They all looked embarrassed. Uncertain.

"You're awesome too," Archie said. "And I have to tell you that I've never seen anybody fall into the river like that and I was scared. So I was really happy when we got down the river and saw Jesse had you."

"Me too," Kyle said.

Tony and Greg said the same.

Robbie came over and laid his head on her shoulder. "Me too." He needed a hug and she gave it to him, meeting Tony's and Greg's gazes over his head.

"I was so proud of all of you. Greg and Tony, you were men out there today, and I know Jesse is going to tell you the same thing when he gets to talk to y'all about it. And you younger boys were great, too. Up until I messed up, you were doing an amazing job. And I'm so proud you did what he asked you to do, when he asked you to do it. Because, see, he was in charge of all of our safety, and his brain was calculating on how to take care of us all. And sometimes the best way to take care of a situation that could get really bad is to just ask you to go along with him, with no questions asked. You did that. You helped him so much by doing that."

Robbie lifted his head. "We ain't always like that."

"No kidding," Tony said. "You caught them on a good day."

They all laughed.

"Well, at least y'all are honest."

Tony gave her a skeptical look. "Confession—that isn't always how it is. Let's go, boys. When Jesse gets here, they're going to have to get settled in. So we need to get out of their hair."

She watched Tony lead by example and head up the stairs. One at a time, they told her goodnight and headed up the stairs after him, each smiling at her.

What a day. They'd all just disappeared up the stairs when she heard Jesse's truck outside. She was tempted to go meet him at the door but he'd given her strict instructions to stay off her feet. She decided that for now, she, too, needed to go along with him. After all, he had rescued her, and she owed him that much.

He walked in the kitchen door and she waved from across the room. His gaze drilled into hers and butterflies trembled in her stomach.

"Are you all alone in there?"

"I am. I just sent them all upstairs. You can go talk

to them, though—they aren't going to bed. Just keeping Mike and Gladys's schedule for tonight. I thought we'd reevaluate together. They are such good boys."

He smiled. "That sounds good. Do you need anything?"

"Oh, no. I've had more coffee, water, and tea…and cookies than any person can handle in an hour's time. To be honest, I'm going to need to head to the bathroom soon."

He grinned as he came around the table. "I can assist you there. And I'm glad the boys were good. They were great. I'll go talk to them after I get you situated."

"Good. And look, my ankle is better."

He sat on the edge of the coffee table and gently took her foot onto his knee. His fingers were gentle as he probed her skin. She was all too aware of the tingles of awareness that raced through her at his touch.

He met her gaze. "Does that hurt? You trembled."

"N-no. It's better."

He let his hand rest on the ankle, his touch light. His hand warmed her skin.

"I'd really like to try to stand on it."

"Are you sure?"

"Yes." She did not need him carrying her around

anymore.

"Okay." He gently placed her foot on the floor then stood. "Let's put your weight on your good ankle first." He held his hands out to her.

She nodded and placed her hands in his.

He smiled. "Put your hands on my forearms and let me put my hands under your elbows to help you keep your balance and not put any weight on that ankle while you get up. Then we'll test the injured ankle."

"That's a good idea." She did as he asked and a moment later, she stood. She kept her hands on his arms for balance. He had his head bent, watching her. Their heads were close as she looked at him.

Her mouth went dry, what was it about this time that they were going through that had them continually in each other's arms or close?

She looked away from him, down at her ankle. "I think I might be able to make it on my own." And then, as she put all of her weight on it, she gasped as pain shot up her leg.

"Okay, maybe I need your arm."

"I'll be glad to help. I was thinking you were being optimistic. But don't lose faith. Maybe tomorrow you can put your weight on it."

"Maybe." She hoped so.

With his arm around her waist and her leaning on

him they made it to the master bedroom.

"I'm thankful the bedroom is on the bottom floor."

"From what I understand, when Mike and Gladys decided early on to make this house into a foster home, they added this room and bath off of the kitchen back here by itself. Mike had wanted a place for Gladys to have some privacy and an oasis from all the boys."

"It's really nice, even after all these years."

"I'm glad you think so. I know it's nothing like what you're used to."

She looked at him. "It's plenty good for me." The bedroom was large and even had a couch in it. And the bath was a nice size also.

She was grateful for its size as Jesse helped her to the bathroom.

"Are you okay?" he asked, stopping at the sink.

She was still holding his arm, even though she could have transferred her hands to the bathroom counter. "Yes. Thank you. I've got it from here. Everything is close enough. I think I can move around using supports."

"You're sure?"

She nodded and loving the feel of his skin far too much, pried her fingers from his arm and placed one hand on the counter and the other on her hip. "I'm good."

"I'll be waiting in the kitchen. Or, if you're going to take a bath, I'll head up and tell the guys goodnight."

"I am going to take a bath, so go up and spend some time with the guys. I'll let you know when I need help from the bathroom to the bed."

His gaze flickered over her face then to the bath. "Take your time. Do you want me to start the tub for you?"

"*No*," she nearly barked in surprise. "I mean, I can do that. Thanks, I'm good now."

He hesitated and the air about them seemed to crackle with electricity. "Okay. I'll be back down soon, so all you have to do is call my name and I'll…" He stepped away from her. "Just call and I'll come get you. Do not try to get from this room to that bed in there. It's too far for you to make it on your own."

He bumped into the doorframe as he backed away from her, and she laughed. It almost looked as if Jesse James were running scared.

"I will call you."

"Okay. At least we won't be cooped up in a tiny room at night together."

She pressed her lips together on that one, holding back telling him she would love to spend the night with him in a tiny room. But that was not the right or helpful response. "Yeah, there is that to be grateful for."

"I'll take the couch, just so you know."

Her stomach tilted. "That sounds good. I hate to take up the whole bed, though."

"We could always share." He winked. "But it's okay, it's easier this way." And then he closed the door behind him.

She just stood there. He was wrong. There was nothing that was going to make this easier.

CHAPTER TEN

He could not sleep.

Jesse lay on the too-short couch, his hands clasped on his chest and his feet hanging over the end of the armrest. The blanket that was supposed to be covering him had slipped once again to the floor. He stared at the ceiling as the reflection of the moonlight played through the windows. Six feet away, Caroline lay in the big bed with her back turned to him. He assumed she was sleeping.

It was nice that one of them was.

He'd known this was going to be hard. But after helping her hobble around, keeping her off her ankle when he'd gotten back to the room, she'd asked him to get her sweatpants, T-shirt, and panties from her suitcase. He'd waited by the door then helped her get to the bed. She'd smelled of sweet-scented soap or lotion, and he'd needed to bang his head against the wall to clear the thoughts he was having from it. Sadly, now it was still full of thoughts that he didn't need to be thinking.

Tomorrow, it was imperative that he get her some crutches. He needed distance between them and that was no joke.

She'd been right when she'd said surely nothing more could happen to them than had happened on their first day of living together. *Torture.* This was, plain and simple, torture.

He forced himself not to think of her snuggled up in that big bed, sleeping soundly. The fact that she wasn't bothered—and he was—irritated him. Then again, what did he expect?

They had such a strange relationship and it boiled down to him.

He flopped to his side with his back to her and stared at the floral couch's back. One of the stiff couch cushions poked him uncomfortably in the side. He gave up and flipped back on his back. That didn't last but a moment before he shifted to his other side and stared at Caroline's back. But, to his surprise, he saw the whites of her eyes across the room briefly before she closed her eyes and her face blended in with the shadows.

She was faking it.

"You can't sleep?" He watched her, waiting for her eyes to show up again.

"I would if I didn't continually hear someone's sighs and groans of...I guess, exasperation. And all that flopping around like a fish out of the water on a pier."

Oh yeah, he was definitely that fish out of water, flopping around in a fight for his life. "This couch is not the most comfortable in all the world."

She sat up. Her hair cascaded over her shoulders, her breasts outlined by the shirt in the shadows. "I'm sorry. I told you I could take the couch. I'm smaller than you. I'd fit better on that couch. Really."

He sat up. He propped his elbows on his knees. He'd had to dig out a pair of cotton pajama bottoms from the bottom of Mike's drawers. Thankfully, he hadn't packed everything up. It was almost as if he'd known Jesse was going to need pajama bottoms.

"I'm not taking that bed. I'll get used to this. It's not really the couch. It's us. I think about us all the time." *What was he doing?*

She leaned her head to the side. "I do, too. But there is no reason for it. You know why. Two days ago, I was broke. Just like you've always wanted me to be. And even then, it was a pretty useless situation for

me because the minute you married me, I'm suddenly not broke anymore. Of course, that depends on if this marriage makes it to the end of three months. So technically, I'm still as broke as you would like me to be."

Her words cut deep and he probably deserved them. "I don't wish you to be broke. But I know that I can never…" *What was he about to say?* He'd never fully opened up to her about his feelings for her and now was not the time. "When I marry for real…if I marry…I want to be able to give my wife things. I know that sounds silly, but a man wants to be able to provide for his wife. But that isn't even the biggest issue. I'm not ready to get married—after we split. Not sure I ever will."

"I don't understand. Why do you think that way?"

"I looked up my parents."

"What?" she asked softly. "You found them?"

"Yeah. You know, being a lawman, you have access to records. That's one of the reasons I became a lawman. I found out that my dad used to beat my mom. She had a long record of being in and out of the hospital with broken bones, bruises, and I found some of my records, too. I don't really remember what I saw there. I remember crying, but nothing much else. It's all shadowy in my mind. I found my mom's trail and it led to the bus station. I don't know what happened to her after that but I was found and taken into the system. I don't know if my mom got on a bus to somewhere. Or if she went back to my dad. I don't know what happened to her. My dad, he went to prison for killing a man. He didn't last long there." *Why had he told her that? He had never told anyone that.*

Caroline ran her hand through her hair and lifted her gaze to the ceiling. "I'm so sorry. And, Jesse, I know what you're thinking. You are not like your dad, so if you're thinking that, then stop."

"I'm not. I know myself, too, and for a brief moment, I thought there was a chance I could have been—in my youth, when I was so rebellious, maybe—but I'm not. I'm like Mike. Praise God. In the end, my mom did what she could for me. I'm not saying dropping a kid off at the bus station is the right thing to ever do. Getting her and me to a safe house would have been best, but maybe she did what she could do in that moment in time. She should have found help for herself and me. Every town has places you can get help. I've made it my mission that every place possible in my county has information posted everywhere. If anyone needs help, there's hotlines, welfare offices. I guess I'm saying that we have helplines everywhere in this town and county. I've made darn sure that if a woman needs help here, they can get it."

"And you've done an amazing job of that. But, Jesse, that still doesn't tell me why you are afraid to get married."

"Maybe I just…" *Can't marry the one I want.* "Just don't have the need to commit to marriage. I'm committing to this boys ranch. To these boys. I want to give them a hundred percent of me. I want to put everything about them first. So, there really isn't any room in my life for a woman."

There, he'd said it. And it rotted in his gut.

"I see. Well, at least now I know the truth. It's out there. I kind of thought that might be what the problem was."

He leaned back on the couch. He rose up, punched his pillow a couple of times, and then reclined again. It was lumpy and uncomfortable and everything felt wrong. "Well, now that we got that out of the way, maybe I can sleep. Do you need anything?"

"No, Jesse, I'm just fine. Sleep good."

He heard her lay back down. Heard the bedding rustle. After a minute, he glanced over and saw her back was to him again.

It was for the best. He closed his eyes and tried hard to wipe her face from his thoughts.

It was a losing battle.

* * *

The morning after the accident her ankle was throbbing but a little better. She woke to find Jesse no longer on the couch and no sign of him having been on the couch. His blanket was gone and anyone who came into the room would never have known he'd slept there—or tried to sleep there.

She thought about the conversation that they'd had and it unsettled her, as it had done when they'd talked. It had been painful for her to hear but then, what had she expected? She'd lain there after they'd gone back to bed; she'd started thinking about how he must have felt when he'd found out about his mother. It must have hurt him terribly. She could tell that he hadn't spoken of it before. Jesse wouldn't. He was a very private guy. But he'd told her.

The very notion that he'd shared that with her pleased her in a small portion of her heart. But she couldn't think about that. He did not want to be a part of her life.

She sat up in bed, wincing as her ankle rebelled. She was going to have trouble getting up and dressed and that was not good news. She was contemplating her next move when the door opened and Jesse stuck his head inside. She was never going to get used to seeing him first thing in the morning in her bedroom.

"You're awake." He entered the room carrying a tray. "I thought you might like breakfast in bed this morning."

Nothing would have surprised her more than this…unless he'd crossed the room and leaned down and kissed her like she longed for him to do.

But no, it was breakfast and a very nice surprise too, his hair was still damp from his shower and his T-shirt was stretched tight across his broad chest and his dark eyes were molten, warm with concern. And everything about the moment had her heart doing a waltz inside her chest.

He leaned down and placed the tray across her lap and his nearness and the subtle scent of soap and spicy aftershave caused her to very nearly melt. When he remained where he was, still holding the tray and looking her in the eyes, he had no idea the war that was waging inside of her. The man's very nearness tempted her far too much. All she had to do was slide her fingers into his hair and grab him by the head and yank him in for that kiss—*okay, get a grip woman!*

He frowned. "Are you okay?"

"What me? Sure, why would you think I wasn't?"

His eyes narrowed. "Because you kind of have a crazed look in your eyes. Are you hurting?"

"Crazed? No," she gave a weak laugh. "My ankle is hurting a bit. Sitting up didn't agree with it. And you did not have to do this. I was about to get up."

"You are not getting up. You've been through an ordeal and I'm going to look at your ankle and then take you in to see Doc Jeffers as soon as the boys get on the bus."

"No, really, I'm fine."

He straightened. "I'm not going to argue about this Caroline. Now, eat your breakfast and I'm going to get the boys on the bus then be back to check on you. And, if I find you out of that bed, I'm not going to be happy. Do you need to go to the bathroom? If so, I can carry you and then bring you back."

Resigned to the fact that he was probably right, she was not going to need to be on her ankle for now, she shook her head. "I'm fine at the moment. You can help me when you get back."

"I won't be long."

And then he was gone. And she was left fretting over the fact that she was injured and not being able to help and worse, she was in a state of turmoil over her reaction to the man. She had to get a grip on her hormones. This was serious business.

Three months. She had to last three months and it hadn't even been a week and she was losing her mind.

He returned a little while later shaking his head. "Whoa, I never herded a bunch of boys through breakfast and out the door before. I have a whole new admiration for what Mike and Gladys did for all these years."

She'd eaten all the eggs and bacon on her plate and had just finished her coffee. She smiled, fairly confident he'd handled everything just fine. Jesse was a very competent in control man. He'd proved that again yesterday when he'd rescued her. "I'm sure you did great. I'm just sorry I didn't get to help you."

He reached for the tray. "You'll get to help soon enough. They were all asking about you. I told them you were okay but that I was taking you in to have your ankle checked out as a precaution."

"I don't need to go in. My ankle isn't broken; it's just tender."

He set the tray on the dresser then returned and knelt beside the bed.

"What are you doing."

"Let's take a look at it. Stick it out here."

"I will not. It's fine." She didn't want his hands on her ankle. The very thought of his hands gently touching her ankle just felt too intimate.

It's your ankle.

Maybe that was silly but that was how she felt.

She did not need—"What are you doing?"

He had pulled the covers up, exposing her ankle and leg. She held her hands on the covers keeping them in place from the thigh up. Of course, she had on shorts but that didn't mean she didn't feel uncomfortable.

"Hold on to your indignation, heiress. I'm just checking your ankle out." He tenderly pressed the skin around her ankle bone. She winced again and tried to hide it but he'd looked at her in that same instant. "Yep, just as I thought. We're going to go see the doctor."

"No."

He stood up and then before she knew what he was doing, he'd slipped his arm beneath her legs and one behind her back and gently scooped her into his arms and started toward the bathroom. "I'll get you in there and grab some clothes for you. Just tell me what you want."

She was in his arms again and getting used to it. "Jesse—" she started to protest but he was already sitting her on the edge of the bathtub.

"Can you manage?"

"I can. Now, just bring my suitcase in here and I can get my own clothes."

"I don't mind getting them."

"Bring my suitcase," she said, giving him a warning glare.

He smiled, looking far too appealing. "I'll do that."

She waited as he went and got the suitcase and carried it into the bathroom. He laid it on the floor in front of her and unzipped it.

"Okay, there you go. I'll carry you out to the truck when you're ready."

The man was not listening. "Jesse, I don't need to go to the doctor. You can help me get to the kitchen when I call you but that's as far as I'm going."

He put his hands on his hips. "You are one stubborn woman."

"Obviously I need to be with all the men trying to run my life these days." It was the truth, she realized. "I do have a brain of my own and free will."

He sighed and hung his head for a second before meeting her gaze. "Okay, I apologize. You're right. I was just concerned. I wasn't trying to run your life. I was just concerned."

"And I thank you for that. But I do have a brain and I will tell you if I need to go to the doctor."

He tipped his hat. "Very well. Just holler when you want me." He waggled his brows then winked at her as he backed out the door and pulled it closed. "I'll be right out here."

She laughed. "Goodbye."

"I heard that," he called.

She shook her head, looked at herself in the mirror and frowned. "Stick to your guns, girlfriend. Do not go weak in his presence or you'll be in more trouble than you already are."

It was true and she knew it.

CHAPTER ELEVEN

Jesse paced in the kitchen as he waited for Caroline to call for him from the bathroom. She was driving him crazy. He picked up his phone and contemplated calling Doc Jeffers. But she'd been right, she was capable of calling the shots when it came to her own body. He set the phone down and walked back into the bedroom. She'd been in there a long time. He was starting to worry she might have fallen down limping around on her injured ankle and hit her head or something. But he hadn't heard a yell or a thud so he forced himself to wait. A second later the door cracked and she stood there holding onto the door knob.

"Okay, I'm ready."

"To go see the doc?"

"Nice try. No, I'm ready to go sit on the porch and prop this leg on a chair it's hurting more after moving around and getting dressed."

"Maybe—"

"Nope, not a word, Jesse James."

He sucked in a disgruntled breath, taking every bit of his will power not to tell her she needed to go see the doctor. Instead he moved to her side. "Fine, lean on me," he said as he slipped an arm around her waist and tugged her against his left side. He was instantly alive with awareness of her.

"Thanks." She wrapped an arm around his shoulder, leaning on him and hopped on her one good foot.

"This is going to take forever if you can't put any weight on it." Not waiting for a reply, he swept her into his arms again.

"Jesse, put me down."

He was starting to like this more and more. He shook his head and said, "I plan to just as soon as I place you in that chair on the porch you were heading to. Then I'll get you whatever your heart desires and let you relax while I work with the horses."

"I'm too heavy for you to be carrying me—"

"Are you saying I'm a weakling? I think I'm insulted."

She laughed. "No, that's not what I was saying but—"

"No buts. I'm plenty capable of carrying you."

"Okay, then. Aren't you going to the office today?"

She was uncomfortable with him carrying her and he knew why. This being close to each other was starting to get to both of them. Before, they could flirt, quip, argue to get rid of the frustrations they felt at being attracted to each other, but then could walk away and accept the reality with distance. It wasn't ideal but it had worked up until now. Now, they were stuck in the house in a marriage with an expiration date on it and they were both struggling. And it hadn't even been a week.

"Well, are you?" she asked again.

He hadn't meant to not answer. "Not today. I'll call and tell them if they need me they can reach me out here. But Clay and Jarred can handle it. Clay is going to be sheriff when I step down anyway, so he might as well get used to it. He'll fill in for the rest of my term and then he'll win in an election with ease. He's a good man."

"True, he is. I am going to need a bit of help getting around. Maybe you can find me a cane. Or a stick I can use."

He pushed the screen door open with his boot and walked out onto the porch. There was a wicker seating area that had been on the porch ever since he could remember. The color had changed through the years, but he was pretty sure as he settled her into the cushioned armchair that it was the same ones.

He realized he hated to let go of her. She smelled of sweet floral scents and he liked the feel of her against him far too much. He placed his hands on the arms and stayed leaning down at eye level. Her pretty green eyes played havoc with his equilibrium drawing him to lean forward when he should be pulling back. "I'll find you something to use. But in the meantime, you just call me and I'll be right here. What do you need right now?"

Her lips parted slightly, and he could so easily lean in and kiss her...he straightened. Stepped back and waited for good measure.

"I'll need my phone, it's on the nightstand beside the bed. And could you bring me my purse? It has my laptop in it."

"Sure thing. Want any coffee or water or tea maybe?"

"Another cup of coffee will be perfect."

"I'll be right back." He headed inside, glad they were back on solid ground. Just where they needed to be.

* * *

Watching Jesse head inside, Caroline breathed a sigh of relief. The man had smelled delicious, of that spicy aftershave he wore—she was certain it was something reasonably priced and not cologne, Jesse wasn't a man to venture too deep into a department store for more expensive cologne and yet he smelled like…perfection. Her head was spinning from his scent and his nearness and she could have stayed in his arms forever. Acting like he wasn't affecting her had taken a huge effort.

She needed a cane or a crutch something fierce and hoped he found her something soon. She would not be able to pretend she was unaffected through much more nearness like that.

She wasn't sure what she was going to do with her time but as he emerged from the house carrying her things, he placed a stack of old magazines on the table with her phone.

"I spotted these in that basket on the hearth and thought it might give you something to look at."

She glanced at the magazines, Good Housekeeping and Southern Living were among them. "Thanks. That's thoughtful of you."

He set her coffee on the table too, and then stepped back next to the steps. He looked as if he was getting ready to run. It was obvious she wasn't the only one having a hard time right now. At least that was good to know since this lie, they lived, of pretending they didn't actually have feelings for each other, was all his fault anyway. If he would just—she shot the thought down without finishing it.

"Call if you need anything. I'll check on you in a couple of hours if I haven't heard from you by then."

"I'll be right here." She picked up a magazine and watched him as he strode down the steps and sauntered across the yard toward the barn. She sighed…the man was as good-looking walking away as he was walking toward her. If she could, she would have whistled…just to tease him. But she couldn't whistle. And it was probably for the best.

She pulled her laptop from her purse and removed it from its leather case. She knew exactly what she was doing with her day today. This rickety chair she was sitting in was on its last leg as was much of the furnishings of this house. And she was about to remedy that. While she was here, there were changes to be made. She was glad that getting married had opened up access to her accounts which was allowing her to do this. When she left, it would be knowing the ranch and the boys' comfort was in a lot better and fashionable way.

* * *

By the time the boys had arrived back home and come walking up the drive from where the bus picked them up and dropped them off, Caroline had had a very busy day on her computer and on the phone talking with retailers. She still had a lot of choices to make and plenty of time to make those choices, but overall she knew by early next week she would have a lot to do. And she didn't need to have this ankle hindering her.

She'd had Jesse carry her to the bathroom twice, and that was because she'd absolutely refused to call him to help her until it was totally necessary. He hadn't lingered over lunch, having settled her on the living room couch with all of her books, and computer and a sandwich and chips that he'd prepared. And a large glass of sweet tea. Because she didn't want to be a bother, she didn't tell him that she normally didn't drink sweet tea but preferred unsweet. She really needed not to have to need him so much and asked him if he'd had time to look for a cane.

Her ankle had continued to throb, and he'd brought her an icepack after catching her grimacing. He hadn't said anything else about taking her to the doctor though. She hoped like everything that she truly didn't need a doctor because she would hate for him to have an I-told-you-so moment to hold over her. Thankfully the icepack helped. And the over the counter painkiller that he also brought with her tea.

After the boys had raided the refrigerator, the younger boys had settled in around her after they'd gotten off the bus and they'd dove into their homework after Jesse told them they could ride over to his place to feed his quarter horses when they were done.

She'd been happy when she was able to help all three of the boys with some of their math questions. Tony and Greg had disappeared upstairs carrying bags of chips and sodas to do their work but returned and headed outside before an hour had elapsed. She hadn't asked them about how their work went, deciding that if they needed help, they'd have asked.

After Jesse and the boys had made sure she was fine and then left for his place, she watched a show on the cooking channel, thinking about what she was going to do when she was able to get up and start doing the cooking. She needed to get a plan in place for that. And that was no joking matter. After the show was over, she realized she'd drank too much tea and needed a bathroom break. Drats. Sighing, she decided this was a good thing. She wasn't going to sit around any longer and she certainly wasn't going to have Jesse carry her around anymore. It was far too frustrating and tempting. Being that close to his tempting lips when he held her in his arms was almost more than she could take.

Besides, she had things to do. She was not going to help these boys by lying around with her ankle propped on a pillow. And the last thing she needed was for Jesse to keep carrying her around like he'd been doing. With her mind set and her determination fired up, she gently set her feet on the ground and then rose to a standing position keeping her weight on her good foot. She looked around the room, determining how she was going to get from the couch to the bathroom, all the way at the back of the house. It was probably going to hurt but since he hadn't found her a cane, she was just going to have to figure this out on her own.

It dawned on Caroline then that in all her shopping that day that she should have ordered herself some crutches. She would do that later tonight and hopefully they would get her one-day delivery or at least by Saturday. But right now, it was hopping time. She hopped across the living room, trying to ignore the pain the hopping was causing the ankle she wasn't using. She reached the dining room table and rested for a moment before she hopped to the kitchen and then rested at the island before she hopped down the hallway and into the bedroom. She was winded and in pain by the time she'd reached the bathroom. She was thankful she had good balance and hadn't fallen flat on her rear. Or face.

Her ankle rebelled but she tried to ignore it. She was not giving in to the pain. She closed the door and sat on the side of the tub before even thinking about making it to the toilet. One thing was pretty clear to her though, hopping around like this was not going to work. At least not for another couple of days until the pain was better. Resigned to the fact that she was going to have to resort to Jesse's help, she opened the bathroom door just as Jesse came barreling into the bedroom looking madder than a grizzly bear.

"Caroline, are you okay?"

"I'm fine. I just needed to use the bathroom and managed on my own. But I have to admit it was a little more of a challenge than I anticipated."

It was then that she noticed he was holding a pair of crutches.

He held them up. "I guess it's a good thing I picked these up while I was in town."

"Yes, thank you!" she gushed, so relieved to see the crutches.

As he walked her way, her heart did a crazy dance in her chest. That was the bad part of all of this. Even knowing that he might like to flirt with her, he was obviously just as attracted to her as she was to him…but he didn't want her. That plain and simple truth was the crux of their entire problem. That and her money. And yet he had the power to drive her crazy with just his presence. Thank goodness for the crutches.

"I called Bernice at the second-hand shop and she said she had a pair. She waited for me at the store before closing to sell them to me."

"I'll have to call and thank her."

"She congratulated us on our wedding and wanted me to be sure and pass that on to you. Thought I better tell you so when you call you'll know to thank her for her congratulations too."

"Thanks for the heads up."

He didn't say anything just stared at her with those dark eyes of his. "Are you sure you're doing okay?"

"I'm fine. But, I'm pretty worn out after all of that so I think I'm going to go ahead and get ready for bed if you don't mind."

"Sure. I'll be in later." He started to leave then paused at the door. "The younger boys really enjoyed you helping them with their homework tonight. I think they…" He looked conflicted.

"What? I loved helping them."

"That's part of what I'm afraid of. When you

leave, what's that going to do to them?"

By Sunday morning, she hated the crutches, was not sleeping well with Jesse sleeping very restlessly on the lumpy couch just feet away from her. She'd been pretending to be asleep every night when he came into the room.

They'd been working together the last few days to keep the boys entertained and to try and figure out how they were silently each maneuvering around each other as they tried to manage living together until the end of the three-month period.

Their conversation from that first night of her accident when they had talked in the darkness had been nagging at her. *I'm committing to this boys ranch. To these boys. I want to give them a hundred percent of me. I want to put everything about them first. So, there really isn't any room in my life for a woman.* Those had been his words but sometimes when he looked at her, she felt…like he wanted more. And she was really having to fight resenting that fact. He judged her by her money and it was starting to burn such a big hole in her gut, that she was having to force back behind a steel door.

He had decided to pretend that they hadn't had that conversation that night. And she was going to go along with it because she really didn't know what else to do.

One thing she did know, her ankle was better. The swelling was down and the throbbing was almost gone. Thank goodness, those crutches were rubbing her underarms raw. They couldn't be tossed too soon for her. She got up, pulled clothes from the dresser where she'd placed the clothes from her suitcase and then went to the bathroom and changed, just in case Jesse were to walk into the bedroom unannounced.

Moments later she maneuvered out into the kitchen to find Jesse pouring a cup of coffee.

"Good morning," she said, eyeing the coffee.

"Good morning. Coffee?"

"You are speaking my language."

"Have a seat on that stool and relax." He set the mug on the counter in front of the first stool.

She moved to it and sat down, propped her crutches against the end of the bar and reached for the hot mug of coffee. The scent filled her with delight as she inhaled and then took a sip. "Amazing."

He chuckled, as he filled another mug for himself then turned to lean against the counter as he took a sip. His warm eyes studied her.

"Did you sleep?"

"It was pretty rocky. Did you?"

"So, so. But this coffee is helping." He took a

drink and their gazes locked over the rim of his mug.

They weren't sleeping because of their proximity to each other.

"Where are the boys?" she asked, yanking her gaze from his and looking around.

"Getting ready for church."

"Oh, right. I must be tired, I forgot."

"It's okay, I'll take them. I wasn't sure if you wanted to go this morning or not with your ankle hurting."

She thought about that as she took another drink of coffee, savoring the rich taste. Her thoughts went to her granddaddy. He would be at church and she might be a chicken, but she was not ready to see him right now. "I think I will stay home this morning. I can get lunch started and have it ready for y'all when you come home."

"Sounds good. I'll have my phone with me, so call or text if you need anything or you change your mind and want me to pick something up. Your ankle isn't completely healed so I can cook tonight. We'll do something on the grill. Maybe some hamburgers."

"That's okay, I'll set some ground meat out for that."

"I'll look forward to it."

"You're already dressed for church. "I must have

been out. You didn't wake me up at all moving around."

He looked over his shoulder and there was a mischievous smile. "You did sound like you were sawing some logs. You couldn't hear me over all the noise you were making. But I am pretty quiet. And I didn't bring my clothes in there last night. I left them out in the kitchen, and I dressed in the guest bathroom."

"I was not snoring," she said indignantly.

"Oh yeah. You were." He started out the door.

"I was not. I do not snore."

He laughed. "You can tell yourself that but you're kidding yourself."

She shot daggers at his back as he moved to the stairs and called the boys.

She did *not* snore. He was just teasing her.

Then again, it wasn't as if she'd ever recorded herself. Maybe he was telling the truth. Maybe she did snore.

* * *

Jesse endured all the slaps on the back and congratulations when he got to church. He hadn't slept much the last several nights. Getting up early was normal for him but now it was necessary. At least he'd gotten her some crutches and was grateful to find them. They were his own form of self-preservation. He didn't need to be tempted by being too close to Caroline after having carried her around on Thursday.

And then there was their conversation the night of her accident. Why had he talked so much? Because she needed to know the score. Needed to know that he wouldn't ever give into the thing they had going on between them.

From his seat near the back of the church, he saw Talbert McCoy in his usual spot in the fourth row. Many of his grandsons and his grandnephews and their families sat around him. He did not go up and sit with them. He might be a church-goer but he was not a hypocrite. He would tell Talbert what he thought about what he was doing to Caroline, but here was not the place to have that conversation.

The preacher preached on patience. He was contemplating what he needed to be patient about, or maybe that sermon was for Talbert—the man needed to be patient when it came to waiting on his grandkids to marry. Him butting into their business was unlike anything Jesse had ever heard of, and when he looked at Ash and Holly and Denton and Blaze and then Caroline's cousins and their wives, it boggled his mind that they'd all been brought together by this off the wall idea of Talbert and his late brother, J.D. Jesse needed patience to deal with the mess he'd gotten himself into and that he was finding was going to be a major problem. Less than a week and he was feeling like he was clinging to a cliff's edge with one toe. His thoughts were so filled with Caroline; he was having trouble seeing anything else.

He found the boys out front with their friends. He could tell that they were telling them about their cattle drive experience and what had happened to Caroline. He started to tell them this morning not to mention it at church but then he decided against it. Word would get out. Him buying the crutches probably had set off a long line of phone calls down the Stonewall gossip grapevine. Besides, for the guys, it had been an exciting moment, and he couldn't deny them the chance to tell their exciting tale. He turned to find someone to talk to and give the boys more time to spend with their friends. He was startled to see Talbert a few feet away.

"Talbert," he acknowledged, keeping his voice reserved.

The older man nodded in acknowledgment. "How's Caroline? I heard that she had an accident at the river."

No surprise there. "I figured word would travel fast when I went down to Bernice's and got those crutches."

"Yes, she called Penny, and Penny called me. I heard one of the boys saying her boot slipped through the stirrup and she got hung up. Would she have made it if you hadn't gone in?"

He saw the worry in Talbert's expression.

"You know Caroline. She is a woman of many talents and determination. She was in a bad way when I got to her, but I believe she would have found a way to get her foot free."

They stared at each other. Jesse tried to breathe shallow and not give Talbert a piece of his mind out here on the lawn. And Talbert, he could tell, was trying not to lose his composure here in public.

"It was that serious, huh? Jesse James, my granddaughter isn't happy right now and to be honest, I'm a little upset with myself. I might have gone a bit too far. But I still don't believe I'm wrong. You give this a shot, son. But even if you don't, you watch out for my granddaughter. You keep her safe. I'd tell you not to hurt her but I'm the one who set her up for this. But one thing I know about my granddaughter is that she is a resilient person. I believe that we'll all come out of this better in the end."

"I hope you're right. But if you're counting on us to remain married, you're going to be disappointed. I have my reasons for my choices, and they won't change just because of something you want. That includes what you're doing to Caroline. It's wrong and you may have lost her for good. Are you prepared for that?"

Talbert's shoulders sank and for a moment Jesse saw disquiet in the old man's eyes.

"Are you?" he asked again.

"One thing I've found in business and in life is that sometimes you think one way, but it's because you don't know what's important. Because you haven't lived life long enough to fully understand what's at stake. Sometimes what we think is important is petty and frivolous. And not quite the obstacle that we think it is."

Talbert didn't get it. Jesse fought down his frustration. "And sometimes people want to tell other people how much more they know about life without caring about how much they hurt that person with their meddling. Anyway, Caroline was up and at 'em this morning and using the crutches and doing better when I left. Her ankle is feeling much better and she's anxious to be a housemother to this brood. You know her—she's out to be the best. She's cooking lunch and settling in now that she can move around a little better. So don't you worry about her. You've driven her to do your bidding but she's going to come out on top. And you're going to be the loser in this."

Talbert dropped his chin to his chest and looked at him from beneath the hat brim. "Did you say my Caroline is cooking lunch?"

It wasn't the reaction he'd expected from what he'd just said to Talbert. "Yes, that's what I said."

"Well, now see, there you go. A good example of pushing boundaries and testing beliefs that one has about oneself."

"And you mean what?"

Talbert laughed. "Son, Caroline can't cook."

CHAPTER TWELVE

Caroline looked at the clock. Church had been over for about thirty minutes, and Jesse and the boys would be driving up soon. She looked at the kitchen and cringed. *What in the world had she been thinking?*

She'd thought, surely, she could cook a simple meal. She'd taken frozen hamburger meat from the freezer and set it in the refrigerator. She then decided to take the flank steak out of the freezer, and fry it up in a pan and slice it. There were some peppers in the refrigerator too, along with a container of cheese sauce in the cabinet and the flour tortillas she found in the pantry. She was going to make fajitas.

But now the fajita meat was burned in the pan, the cheese sauce was a nasty burned conglomeration, and the tortillas were dried out and hard as bricks. And the peppers looked awful and unappetizing in the pan that she'd tried to sauté them in. It was all a disaster, and the kitchen was full of smoke from the burned meat.

And now Jesse and the boys were going to come through that door at any minute and see her mess. She hobbled over to the door on her crutches and pulled the door open wide to let the smoke start to escape. She coughed and went back to the stove and picked up the now cooling pan of burned meat. She couldn't hobble on two crutches and carry a pan outside, so she left one crutch leaning against the counter and then used the one on her injured ankle's side as she slowly made her way out onto the porch and down the steps. She was only a few steps from the porch when Jesse drove up the drive and parked. She froze, caught in the act. She watched them all climb out of the truck. Jesse was carrying two big paper bags.

He held them up. "I've decided that you didn't need to cook on your first day and with those crutches, so I picked up a bunch of tacos, chips, and salsa. Does that sound good?" He glanced toward the house, where smoke could be seen drifting from inside. "Is everything okay in there?"

"Yes, it's fine. And tacos sound perfect."

All the guys came toward her, smiling and teasing.

"We heard at church that you don't know how to cook." Robbie grinned.

Tony came and took the pan from her. "Want me to toss this over the fence? I'm assuming that's where you were heading."

"Yes, Mr. Smarty Pants, that's where I was going. I was trying to get rid of the evidence before all of you got home."

"I've got this." He grinned, took the pan, and strode quickly to the fence and tossed the meat on the pasture side for some wild animal to come up and devour.

Archie smiled. "It's okay. Gladys tried to teach me how to bake cookies, and I burned them all up."

"I did too," Greg confessed. "But I wasn't really trying. Gladys bakes great cookies, and I didn't want her telling me to go in there and bake cookies when I knew mine were never going to be as good as hers."

She laughed and shook her head. "Well, you know, guys, I was trying to do something I've not been able to do before, and it kicked my rear. But you know what? I think that I'll get better. And if y'all can have some patience, I think that I'm not going to give up. What do you think? Will you hang in there with me?"

The guys looked at each other, shrugged, and grinned.

Tony spoke for them. "We're in. But on the way here, Jesse told us that he knows how to cook, so maybe he can help."

Her jaw dropped and she glared at Jesse, who grinned. "So, you can cook more than breakfast?"

He walked forward, swinging the bags of tacos. "I didn't want to brag or anything, and sometimes it's not always good to show all your cards at one time. Hey, I was a bachelor. If I didn't want to live off store-bought food, then I had to up my cooking game. And Gladys is a good teacher and always tried to teach the boys some skills." He looked at Greg and Tony. "Just some guys didn't want to learn."

"Hey," Tony said. "I never said I couldn't cook."

"Ahh, so now we're getting somewhere. So, here's the deal, fellas. Caroline and I can't do it all. Sooo, we are going to have to chip in and make this happen. Maybe we can all help each other out."

They all chimed in with agreement. Caroline was fascinated. Her disaster was turning into something great. "Now, can we eat? Maybe we should do it over there on the picnic table. The house is really smoky."

Tony headed toward the house. "Sounds good to me. I'll take this in and put it in the sink. And grab some utensils, paper plates, and a pitcher of tea and glasses, then be right out."

Jesse watched him disappear into the house then looked at her. "That kid has potential."

"Tell me about it. I think he'll be able to teach me

a bunch of things."

"Come on, let's sit down and hand these out. We've got some hungry boys."

She started toward the table, moving slow with the single crutch. He had made it to the table and set the bags on it and then turned to see she was moving slower than him.

"I'm kind of slow."

He came back to her. "That looks almost painful."

She paused with her weight on the crutch. "It's not terrible when I have both of them. It's just hard using one. I couldn't carry the pan with the burned meat and two crutches at the same time."

He hesitated then offered his arm. "Let me assist. I'll be your second crutch over to the table, then I'll get your other one after you're comfortable with a taco in your hands."

She hesitated, then linked her arm in his. "Thank you."

"My pleasure." They moved slowly toward the table.

The boys were running around the house, chasing Shaggy. She laughed at their antics.

* * *

Jesse was conflicted about telling her about his

encounter with Talbert. "I saw your granddaddy at church."

"I thought he would be there."

"He was worried about you. He'd heard about the accident."

She paused. "He has a terrible way of showing it."

"I know what you mean. I told him what he's doing to you is wrong. He really made me angry and I told him he may have gone too far with you."

Pain filled her expression. "He did go too far. There are some things that can't be taken back. He was very deceptive and hurtful."

The boys raced by and the dog barked. Robbie fell down and the dog pounced on him, and they rolled around, all giggles and laughs.

She sighed and looked back at Jesse. "I love that. Come on. Let's pass out some tacos and no more talk about my granddaddy."

"I'm on board with that. Come on, just a few more feet. You're really slow."

She bumped him hard with her shoulder. "And you're rude."

"But I saved the day—twice. And by dinner time it will be three times...I take that back—it'll be four times. Crutches, breakfast, lunch, *and* dinner."

She laughed. "Okay, fine. You win. But these

tacos better be awesome."

It did his heart good to hear her laugh. "Oh, they will be. Sit and be amazed. Come on, boys. Taco time."

Tony had reached the table with his pitcher of tea and glasses. The rest of the guys scrambled onto the picnic table bench seats, leaving the only spot for Jesse beside her.

"May I?"

He could see she wanted to tell him to squeeze in on the other side of the table but the four boys crammed in across from her would probably not like that idea. "Sure. Why not."

He laughed and sat beside her. "Yeah, total torture. I totally get it."

"Funny. Real funny."

* * *

After the boys got on the bus for school on Monday morning Jesse was about to get into his truck when Caroline had come out onto the porch and waved. He'd paused with his hand on the door of his truck and fought the urge to go over and see her before he left. She looked fresh and pretty and when she'd smiled and called out for him to have a good day it had taken a herculean effort to wave and climb into his truck and head to work.

It was the best course of action. He'd taken some time off but he was still the Sheriff, but now he needed to make some final decisions about his job.

But his mind was on Caroline as he drove, not his job. She had been getting around better at breakfast. He'd cooked the bacon and eggs and she'd made the toast. He laughed thinking about her lack of cooking skills. She was brilliant with a paintbrush but really bad in the kitchen. But that didn't seem to matter to the boys who absolutely loved her and she them. Thanks to her, there had been a lot of teasing and loud, laughing conversations at breakfast and each boy had gotten a hug and a warm smile and encouragement before leaving for the bus. Even Tony and Greg hadn't minded at their age. He'd been envious…then again, he'd had another sleepless night.

Every night had been that way from night one. He had once again lain awake staring up at the ceiling with the pestering wish that she would stop pretending to be asleep and start a conversation. But she hadn't rolled over on her side and talked again. He assumed she'd thought they'd said enough the first night. And another late night conversation was not what they needed.

Opening up to her like that made no sense.

He took care of some paperwork in the office, set up the schedule for the week and then made a few rounds in town.

By the time Jesse got back to the ranch that afternoon, he was beat. There had been a wreck on I-35 and they'd had to use the jaws of life to cut the man out of the truck. Jesse was thankful it hadn't been worse. The man was just going to spend a few days in the hospital before getting to go home. Jesse always liked a happy ending.

It was an odd feeling knowing that he was about to not be a lawman. It was a part of his life that was hard to give up, but he wanted to give his full attention to the boys and the ranch. And therefore, he had given his two-week notice and his main deputy was stepping in to take over for him.

He drove up to the house and parked the truck. Caroline was on the porch. She was moving around, hobbling and using a broom to sweep with and to help her not put too much pressure on her ankle. He smiled as he watched her. She'd said her ankle felt better this morning. He got out of the truck and strode toward her.

"Please tell me you aren't trying to burn the house down again."

"No, I am not." She shot him a good-natured

glare. "I'm just cleaning up out here a little bit. I've ordered a few things to spruce the place up. Hopefully Gladys won't mind. I won't be here long, but I can leave the house in much better shape than I found it."

She didn't even sound disturbed that she wouldn't be here. She'd come to terms with it. It didn't settle well with him. He was not happy with that. It was as though he wanted one thing but then didn't. "Sure. I think those wicker chairs have been there since I was a kid. Gladys spray-painted them a few times to make them look good but they're getting pretty wobbly."

"That's what I think. And you do know that I like to put my touch on things. So, since I have access to my accounts now that we are married, I'm going to use them. There will be a few deliveries over the next few days."

That was so Caroline. "I see you were really interested in my opinion, since you've already made the calls."

She held her hands up and smiled impishly. "So, sue me. A girl has got to do what a girl has got to do. Especially if she doesn't have long. Women tend to like change."

And ugly churning started in his gut. "It's your money—do what you want with it. I'm sure it will be appreciated." Instead of going onto the porch, he rested his forearms on the railing and looked up at her as he fought off the negative reaction. She was doing a good thing.

"I need to start going through the books and see where the ranch stands. We're going to draw up papers and agree on a fair market price after they get back. But Mike gave me all the financials to look over, so I'll have a better understanding of the whole picture."

"You've already agreed to take over and you don't know the price?"

"That sums it up. Mike's a fair man, and I want this."

She sat down on the wicker chair and studied him as if he were from an alien planet. "Wow."

He felt uncomfortable. "Before you start thinking I'm a total loser at business, that is all irrelevant to me. I'm in this for the boys. And so are Mike and Gladys. I'm going to go over everything closely so that I know what I have to deal with. I want to make the place independent and not reliant completely on the purse strings of philanthropists like you."

Her expression flattened, as if she'd taken a slap to the face. "Oh...you know I'll give whatever you need. I've tried to give more but Mike would only take what he needed. I think he didn't want the ranch to be reliant on just one investor, so he took a little from everyone in hopes, like me, they'd always be there to help. As if he worried he'd take advantage of someone and they'd turn their giving off."

"Like your granddaddy did. I think you're absolutely right about what they were doing. And there is some stress doing that—being dependent on donations. He had a healthy-looking exterior but he was a man with a lot on his shoulders all these years."

"You're right. I never thought about that."

"I didn't either, not completely. I thought about trying to make it self-sustaining, but I didn't think about the full responsibility until it settled onto my shoulders. I woke this morning and it hit me. It's heavy. See, if you were to pull out, or the money dried up from the other investors, this ranch wouldn't make it. And that means these boys would be displaced again and sent to other foster homes. Mike did tell me that the money the state gives them per boy only covers their clothes and food, basically. There isn't anything extra. It certainly wouldn't cover upkeep and taxes on the ranch.

"Even if it was owned outright, there are expenses. The land has to be looked after and maintained. It's expensive but worth it. I love this place. It's special. And a house on a lot or an acre of land wouldn't be the same. It's not big by McCoy standards, but being able to run free out here and have this lifestyle is a lot for a kid who came from a bus station with nothing to his name. It was a blessing. It means everything to me, and I need to pay this forward. All guys who called this home feel the same way."

Caroline had listened to him with a soft expression on her face. Now she gave him a sincere smile. "I always knew you were the right one to take over. Your heart is in the right place and it's that way because you lived it. I get it now. A week ago, I didn't, but Granddaddy opened my eyes about a lot of things when he cut me off. I need to be independent and viable on my own, and so does this ranch. As much as I love giving to it and will do so as long as needed, it would be healthier for it and the boys here if it could do well on its own."

"And it will be. I just need to figure out a way to support this place, and I'm not going to be able to do that on my sheriff's salary. So, I have some ideas and I'd like to run them by you when I get them all together." He was putting himself out there. *What if she laughed at his ideas?* He shut that train of thought down, because this was about the boys. Not his pride.

Her expression brightened. "I would like that. I'd like that a lot."

The way she was smiling at him, he felt

181

encouraged. She got what he was worried about, and she understood and agreed that the ranch needed to be self-sufficient as much as possible. He was rather hesitant about talking about his ideas. And getting her thoughts and ideas too. Maybe together, they could figure this out.

* * *

The boys arrived home from school and they were glad to be home. They marched into the house, piled their backpacks on the small bench in the hall, and then headed into the kitchen and flopped into the chairs around the table and at the kitchen island. Caroline smiled as she pulled open the refrigerator feeling good that today she'd been able to actually do some things for them. She pulled out a fresh pitcher of sweet tea and the two large trays of cheese and fruit that she'd prepared earlier. She couldn't cook, however, she knew how to go to the grocery store and she could slice cheese and make a fruit tray as good as anyone—and there was no smoking oven involved.

"I thought these would be good snacks." She set one on the counter where Tony and Greg were sitting and she placed one on the table for the younger boys. "Who wants tea?"

"Thanks," they all echoed each other as hands went up then immediately went back down as they needed two hands each to stack large quantities of cheese on crackers.

Watching them made her smile and her heart swell. She had been afraid they'd balk at the idea but before she'd turned to get the glasses out, they'd seemingly eaten half the platters.

Jesse was already pulling out plastic glasses when she turned around.

"I'll fill these with ice while you pour." He held a glass under the ice maker on the refrigerator and started filling it with ice.

"Teamwork…I like it." She took the glass of ice he held out to her; their fingers brushed and electrified butterflies inside her stomach.

"Me too." He hesitated, as if he were going to say more, then put the other glass under the ice spout.

She poured tea in the glass and set it in front of Robbie. It only took a couple of minutes to have tea for each kid, and then he held a glass out to her.

"For you, and one for me."

"Thanks." The boys had gotten the initial after-school hunger calmed down and were eating a bit slower by then.

Robbie said, "I had a really good day at school

today. I told my teacher that you and Caroline are taking care of us while Mike and Gladys take a vacation, and I told her y'all were doing a great job."

"That's sweet of you." Caroline was touched and grabbed a piece of cheese and a cracker.

He beamed at her. "She asked me if y'all were coming to the open house tomorrow?"

Jesse looked confused. "Open house?"

"Yeah, where you get to meet my teacher and see my artwork." Robbie grinned. "I colored a good one."

"I'm glad you told us, Robbie. I think Mike and Gladys forgot to tell us, they were so excited about going on their vacation. I'll check on it in the morning and we'll for certain be there for all of you."

"It's right after school," Tony said.

"Thanks for telling us. We wouldn't miss it for the world." Caroline looked around the room and wondered whether it bothered the boys that they didn't have parents coming. Her granddaddy came to the meetings after her parents died. The memory caused a pang of regret, thinking about him. "Did you have to do special artwork or anything to show off for us?"

"Not us." Greg wagged a thumb from Tony to him then nodded at the smaller boys. "But I bet they did."

"Yep. I painted a wagon train." Archie grinned. "It's not great but you can tell what it is. And believe me that's a big deal."

"That's me too. I painted a horse but it looks like a dog." Kyle hooted with laughter and everyone joined in.

"I painted a house. This one," Robbie said when the laughter quieted down. "I like it here."

Jesse met her gaze, and she felt the weight of his desire to make life better for these boys. She looked away, knowing she was going to really have to not let her heart get overwhelmed with the feelings so easily evoked by merely meeting his eyes or listening to his heart…which was what she'd listened to out on the porch earlier. When he spoke of making this ranch dependent on no one but himself, he was speaking out of love because he wanted to protect these boys.

She could admire him. She could help him. But she could not let herself drop the shields to her heart.

CHAPTER THIRTEEN

There was tension between them the next morning. He was gone when she woke so she sat up in bed, feeling groggy and uptight as she glanced around the room. Haphazard sleep was wearing on her.

They'd had a good evening yesterday after learning of the surprise open house, parent-teacher meeting. The boys had gone out to do their chores, the younger boys taking care of the animals in the barn and the older boys taking the truck out to feed the cattle cubes in the pastures. Jesse had cooked chicken on the grill and she'd put frozen corn on the cob into boiling water and opened some cans of beans. It wasn't fancy but at least she got her part done without smoking the house up. The boys continued to tease her relentlessly while they ate and everyone got a good laugh about it. It was a very fun dinner and she was glad her mishap gave them something to bond over. The boys also brought up staying up an hour later, and she and Jesse had agreed that they could. Part of their unspoken reasoning was that that would give them an hour more a night that they wouldn't be alone.

As bedtime had gotten closer, her thoughts had gone back to having to sleep in the room with him every night. It had been a week and they'd managed but neither of them were really sleeping, and there was an air of unease in the room every night.

Last night had been rough. After the boys had gone upstairs, an hour later than usual since she and Jesse had agreed that would be okay, as had become their routine, Jesse had gone to check on the horses and she'd gone to get ready for bed. She'd dressed in her warmups and T-shirt, she'd climbed into bed and pretended to be asleep when he'd come in nearly an hour later. Lying in bed, she'd kept her back to him, hoping that if she did so, they wouldn't end up talking again like that first night. And like every other night, she'd lain there listening to him tossing and turning on the couch while her thoughts filled with wishes and wants that she had no business thinking about because it only caused her misery.

She felt sorry for him but she knew the couch was the safest place for him.

Pushing herself to shake it off, she dressed, put on her game face and walked out into the kitchen. And straight into Jesse as he was coming out of the pantry.

"Ouch," she gasped and fell back, off-balanced when she tried to catch herself.

In an instant Jesse dropped the paper towels in his hands and grabbed her by the arms. She fell against him and for that moment they were locked together. She stared up into his strong, handsome face. She couldn't move, only take in the look of him, the feel of him and that scent of spicy aftershave and clean fresh soap that was quickly becoming an intoxicating trigger for her body. Her heart pounded, her pulse raced and she could not move.

His eyes dug into hers, intense and heated and then, in a blink it was gone. "Sorry, I didn't see you. Did I hurt you?"

"N-no," she swallowed hard, lost in his eyes as she searched for that spark he'd just doused. His hands burned her skin reminding her how weak her resolve was when he touched her. Reminding her that she too needed shields up. "I'm fine, Sheriff. But maybe you need to write yourself a ticket for reckless walking." She forced a chuckle and then took a step back. He released her and she fought a bitter battle not to throw herself back into his arms.

Have some pride, girlfriend.

Thankfully the voice in her head was thinking straight.

His lip twitched. "I'll start looking before I cross." He bent down and picked up the new roll of paper towels that were lying at her feet.

His dark hair brushed her hand. Her reaction to the simple contact was as strong as his touch. Her stomach felt bottomless and her pulse raced. She was so fiercely attracted to Jesse that she knew she was in a no-win situation right now. But she was not giving in.

"I need coffee." She headed to the coffee maker…escaped was more like it.

"I made plenty. I've scrambled a skillet of eggs and sausage too."

"Great. I'll get the orange juice," she said as she poured her coffee and then took several sips praying it would help put her back on stable ground. The boys thundering down the stairs like a heard of mustangs broke the spell somewhat and she went to the refrigerator and pulled out the OJ. She poured orange juice in glasses and made toast while the boys were in and out rushing through the kitchen and to the laundry room searching for socks and shirts. She realized only then that she hadn't ventured into the laundry room not once the entire week. She looked inside and nearly fainted when she saw the baskets of clothes.

"What is all that?" she asked Tony who was digging in one of the baskets.

"Bingo," he said, holding up two matching socks like they were an Olympic medal. "The laundry. We kinda slacked on folding it. Sorry."

"So those baskets are clean clothes?"

"Yes. Our dirty clothes are still upstairs."

She cringed as memories of three brothers' laundry slammed into her. "Okay, good to know. Maybe we should attack that tonight."

Greg squeezed past them. "I hate laundry, it never ends."

She laughed. "Believe me, I know. I had all those brothers growing up. I've been on my own for a few years and had just forgotten how bad it could be." It was so true. But life growing up with her brothers flooded back and she had a new appreciation for her grandmother and granddaddy.

Her thoughts went to her grandmother and her morning ritual before they all raced from the house to catch the bus and later to jump into their cars. She smiled and her heart swelled with love for her sweet grandmother. They'd lost her several years ago. Caroline never would forget getting that call from Granddaddy during her first year of college. The woman had meant so much to her. One strong memory stood out and Caroline smiled and a few minutes later when the boys finished eating, she positioned herself at the door just like Grandmom had done. Then, she gave each of the boys a hug before they raced from the house. She and her brothers had lost their parents, but they never left for school without knowing they were loved. While she was here in this house she was going to pass that on to these boys.

Little Robbie hung back and was the last one in line. When she hugged him, he hung on tight and she was so thankful for her grandmother's love…and her granddaddy's too, but she still wasn't ready to think about that this morning.

Instead she hugged Robbie tight. "Have a good day, okay. We'll see you after school at the meet the teacher event. I can't wait to see your picture."

He grinned. "Great." And then he raced out the door, jumped from the porch to the ground and ran as fast as his legs would carry him down the lane to the waiting bus.

She watched him, her heart tight. When she turned, Jesse was watching her with an intensity that shook her.

"I'm glad I'm here," was all she could say as she straightened to a standing position.

He nodded, his gaze softening. "Thanks for being here...for the boys." He cleared his throat. "Well, I need to go get my horses and bring them out here and then head to the office. Have a good day." He walked past her and out onto the porch. He paused and looked back, catching her still watching him. "What are you doing today?"

She knew the score, that they had no real future together and yet as she stared at him, she was startled by how much she wanted to shake sense into him. How much she wanted him to look at her and see her and not all the money. But that wouldn't happen, she had money and she was using it. "I'm cleaning and getting ready for trucks bearing good things."

He looked thoughtful. "That's right." He looked at the old porch furniture then at her, something flat in his eyes. "I'm sure you'll enjoy that."

She didn't exactly like the flatness of his eyes or his words. She sighed as he strode to his truck. She forced herself not to watch him leave. She had things to do and so what if she enjoyed decorating and shopping?

This was a good thing. This place had probably never had an update since the day it was built. And that was changing starting today.

CHAPTER FOURTEEN

Jesse swung by and picked her up then they headed back to town. He hadn't come inside since he'd been held up at the office and was running late. Thus, he hadn't seen the changes she'd been working on all day. The trucks came and she'd had an exciting and exhausting day moving furniture around.

Now, feeling nervous, she walked beside Jesse into Robbie's classroom, having decided to go from youngest child to oldest in order of which teachers to see first. Her ankle had gotten better during the day and though it hurt some she was only limping slightly.

Mrs. Smith looked up from where she was organizing papers and her eyes warmed. She was one of the oldest teachers at the rural school and had taught her as well as Jesse.

"Caroline and Jesse, come in. I'm just so thrilled

for the two of you and want to first say congratulations on your wonderful, though sudden, marriage. Penny tells me that she'll be hosting a reception for you as soon as all the arrangements can be made. I'm looking forward to celebrating with you both. And the boys are so excited."

Beside her, she felt Jesse stiffen. Or maybe she stiffened. She'd known this was coming but had hoped Penny wouldn't start plans without first asking her. Now she tried to compose herself enough to answer, because Jesse was as silent as she was while Mrs. Smith smiled warmly from her to him.

"And we're excited to celebrate with everyone. I'm just not sure it will happen anytime soon. We…we're focusing on helping out with the boys right now. And so we're here to talk about Robbie. He's such a sweet boy and we want to make sure he's doing well. That's why we've come a little earlier, hoping to talk before other parents and guardians come in. He's waiting out in the hall for us before we call him in."

"He's excited to show us his artwork." Jesse's gaze connected with hers, and she felt as though he were relieved by her statement.

The teacher smiled in agreement. "I believe that is a wise choice. Robbie is pleased about you two being there. He's a sweet boy and seems to be adjusting well.

He works hard in class…almost…" She hesitated, then gave a sympathetic sigh. "Almost as if he's afraid if he messes up, there will be consequences."

Caroline didn't understand. She looked at Jesse for answers. His mouth had settled into a flattened line. Meeting her gaze, his dark eyes held hers, and she saw the battle inside.

"Yes, ma'am, I expect he probably worries, that no matter what assurances he's gotten, that his life at the ranch could be yanked out from under him if he messes up."

Caroline got it then. "Poor kid." She'd never doubted her granddaddy's love and the security of her home with him after losing her parents. But it hit home now that these boys didn't have that assurance. "I didn't realize."

He placed a hand on her shoulder and gently squeezed. "You couldn't have known. Me, I should have realized it. I lived it and so did all the boys who were at the ranch when I lived there. It took us all time to realize that Mike and Gladys weren't going to give up on us and send us away. I'm sure the older boys understand that. But the younger ones might not. Robbie, especially."

"Yes, I've seen it many times over the years. Gladys and Mike loved all you boys like you were their own, and I believe you each eventually relaxed in the security of their love. I believe Robbie will get there, too. I just felt like I should make you aware of my observation."

"Thank you," Caroline said, feeling grateful. "I will make sure he starts feeling secure."

"I know you will. You have deep empathy, Caroline. I remember watching you at a young age taking up for anyone who might be bullied or who needed a friend. You have been born with money but you've always been generous. You have a good heart, and I truly believe you'll be good for the children." She looked from one to the other. "Gladys is my friend, and she confided in me that you two were permanently taking over the ranch because they needed to retire for Mike's health and hers."

"Oh." Caroline breathed the word, shocked but also touched by Mrs. Smith's words. She felt guilty that not everything Gladys had said was true. She wasn't here permanently.

"I know you'll keep that confidential until they've come back and told the boys." Jesse shifted his stance, and she wondered whether he was as uncomfortable with the lie as she was.

"Of course. I just thought you should know that I understand, and I believe that Robbie will grow more comfortable as time passes, though I can't be sure how their leaving is going to affect him. He may feel like once again his life is uprooted by someone leaving. So if you'll be aware of this and understanding, it will be helpful."

"We will be," Caroline assured her and knew that she would do everything she could to help Robbie and all the boys. And she hoped that, in the end, when she left, it didn't do any damage to them emotionally.

Other parents were now coming in and Mrs. Smith excused herself to go greet them. She and Jesse stared at each other for a moment.

Jesse spoke first. "Let's bring Robbie in, and we'll discuss the evening later, after we've visited all the teachers."

"I think that's a good idea."

They went and found Robbie talking with several boys. He was excited to come inside and take them to a wall of art. He pointed his out.

It was a simple drawing in crayon of a big house with a wide porch; flowers were in the yard and so were five small people and a dog. And on the porch was a woman with long blonde hair and a man wearing a badge.

He smiled up at them. "We were supposed to draw something that made us happy. I didn't know what to draw and I stared at the paper for a long time. And then I thought about the ranch. That's the ranch house and y'all on the porch, and me and the boys in the yard with Shaggy."

Caroline's heart squeezed hard and she knelt, the skirt of the dress she'd worn pooling on the floor around her. "Robbie, I love this. I love it so much. I'm so glad we, and the ranch, make you happy. Because you make us happy."

Jesse placed a hand on her shoulder and knelt on one knee as he placed his other hand on Robbie's shoulder. "Caroline is right about everything. Especially the part that you make us happy. And this is the best picture. I'm glad the ranch makes you happy."

Robbie beamed and then threw his arms around Caroline's neck and hugged her tight.

Tears welled up before she could stop them, and she squeezed her eyes shut as she hugged the small boy tightly. She was startled when she felt Jesse's thumb gently wipe the tears from her cheeks. She opened her eyes and met his gaze over Robbie's shoulder. He smiled at her and there was a bittersweet edge to it. They were in public; people were probably looking at them. But right now, none of that mattered. This little boy and the fact that he understood that her heart was full and hurting at the same time was what mattered.

Gathering her composure, she looked at Robbie. "Okay, so are you ready to go see what the other boys have been up to?"

"Yes, I bet they did good too." He grinned.

"I like your positive attitude," Jesse said, rubbing the kid's head as they started for the door.

They were almost to the door when Mrs. Smith called out to them. They halted as she came back their way.

"I meant to ask you both if you were ready for the fall festival a week from Saturday?"

"What festival?" Caroline asked.

"Oh, dear, they didn't tell you?" Mrs. Smith looked dismayed.

"Tell us what?" Jesse asked.

Looking worried, Mrs. Smith clasped her hands together. "The school has our fall festival every year and the parents or guardians help out with booths. Mike and Gladys had signed up to oversee the three-legged race. You will be there, right? At this late date I'm not sure I can find someone else and it's a very popular event."

"It'll be fun," Robbie said, looking excitedly at up at them.

Jesse smiled from Robbie to Mrs. Smith. "Of course, we will help. You just tell us what we need to do, and we'll do it."

"Great. I knew I could count on you. See you Saturday after next. Oh, and bring a cake for the raffle."

"A cake, sure," Caroline said, feeling like if this kept up she was going to have to hire a cook for the ranch…something she was pretty sure Jesse would not go for. She sighed and caught his eye as they left the room. She leaned close as they walked down the hall behind Robbie. "Does it count if I buy the cake?" she asked softly.

He leaned closer. "I can try to help on that but my baking skills are not as good as my grilling skills. We might need to bring in the troops. Doesn't someone in your family bake?"

She smiled, feeling relieved. "I'm sure I can talk one of my girlfriends in to helping out. If not, then Nelda, Wade and Allie's housekeeper, could probably help us out."

They smiled at each other.

He looked as relieved as she felt. "Thanks for being here," he said. "It means a lot to me. To the boys."

"I'm glad to help." And she meant it.

She also knew it felt right.

So very right to be here.

* * *

Later, after they finished with the teacher meetings, Jesse drove them home but first stopped by the store and picked up a couple of cartons of ice cream for them to enjoy when they got home. A celebration for the boys that their teachers had had nothing but praise for them and a celebration for Jesse and Caroline that they only had to bake one cake and run one booth at the upcoming fall festival.

The meetings had gone well, but he'd felt deceptive, very deceptive when Mrs. Smith had talked with them. He felt like Caroline had the same feelings. He told himself it couldn't be helped. This was the way it had to be, the way they'd agreed it would be.

But that hadn't meant he hadn't been feeling uncomfortable about the whole thing and with each teacher they saw the feeling had grown. Caroline had been talkative with the boys all the way home but there had been something in her face that made him think she too was bothered.

They all walked into the house and he set the bag of ice cream on the counter. He was at the sink washing his hands before dishing up the ice cream when he heard gasps.

"Wow," Tony said.

And the others made similar comments.

He turned to see what was going on and they were all lined up looking into the living room. He saw it then, the transformation. He'd forgotten all about Caroline's trucks. She was standing to the side smiling and watching the boys.

The room was completely changed. Gone was the ancient floral couch and the plaid chairs. In their place was a huge sectional situated in a completely different direction from the way the couch and chair had been set up. There was a massive wooden wall cabinet with a new large flat-screen television with speakers and what looked like surround sound. And colorful pillows on the couch and a new rug.

"Is this for real?" Greg asked, his expression one of complete awe.

No one had moved yet. They all turned to look at him. He hadn't known what he'd expected from her but his mind hadn't fully grasped what she was capable of. He had expected maybe a couch, but this was top of the line, magazine makeover type stuff. He saw the disbelief in their eyes and the excitement too.

He fought down the feelings of inadequacy welling up inside of him and pointed at Caroline. "You have Caroline to thank for that."

She looked delighted as the boys, almost giddy as

she clapped her hands together and held them under her chin. "I tried really hard to get something I thought you'd love. Go on, go try it out and I hope you like it."

"Yes. It's totally cool," Kyle said and then raced into the room and sank down on the sectional. Robbie and Archie laughed and did the same.

"It looks comfortable. And I like the brown color," Greg said, grinning. "But that flat-screen is awesome."

Tony looked pleased and as usual was more laid back. "Thanks. Can I turn it on?"

"Sure, the remote control is on the shelf. If you can't figure it out just holler. We'll get the ice cream ready while you two bright young men figure out the television."

The two older boys grinned and went to check out the new electronics as Caroline turned to face him. Her excitement faded as she looked at him.

"You don't like it?"

"It's nice." He went back to the cabinet and pulled out the bowls. He told himself to let this pass. She had not cut corners but had spent a lot and it had hit him hard how easy it was for her to make changes since anything she wanted was at her fingertips. It hadn't registered to him how old everything in the house was or how little Mike and Gladys had spent on sprucing the place up. They had been frugal and good stewards of the donations received and he admired them for that. But looking about the place now, he knew it was long past time that things be updated. And now that she had the chance, after all the times she'd offered to give them more and they hadn't taken her up on it, Caroline was making sure this place had a makeover before she left. Because she cared and she had walked into the house and seen the need.

She came to stand beside him. "You really don't like it."

He heard dismay in her words. Maybe hurt. It bothered him that he hadn't recognized the need. And it bothered him that he hadn't been able to do it himself. He'd struggled with the feelings. She had the money and could do this. But her walking into his world and immediately seeing what was lacking showed exactly how far apart their worlds were. And how lacking he was on what he could ever offer her.

"I do like it. It all looks great. I just hadn't expected so much."

"I see. Well, they deserve it and it was needed. Now, when I'm gone, you won't have to do it again for a very long time."

"Yeah, I guess you have a point." They stared at each other and he felt as far out of her league as he ever had.

Her excitement had faded. "Well, stay tuned, there are more changes coming. As you are aware, my skills fail me in the kitchen, but I can shop and that's just what I'm doing while I have the chance." A cheer went up from the boys as the television came on full blast. She smiled, somewhat bittersweet. "At least some people appreciate my skills."

She left him then, walking into the living room to join in the talk and laughter of the boys as they chattered excitedly.

He felt like a jerk.

When bedtime rolled around, Robbie asked Caroline if she would read to him before bedtime.

"Sure, I'd love to," she said, sliding from the stool she'd been sitting on. She looked at Archie and Kyle, who also shared a room with Robbie. "How about it, boys, I bet I can find a book you'll all like."

Kyle got a comical wary look. "Not a baby book though."

"And no fairy tales," Archie added, just as wary.

She laughed and Jesse's heart sighed at the sound. He'd always liked her laugh.

"I promise." She glanced at him and the older boys. "Y'all are welcome to come for story time too."

Tony and Greg looked so horrified that Jesse had to laugh. "It's okay, we'll hang out and talk. I need to ask their advice on a few things."

"Okay, but you three have no idea what you're missing. Come on, fellas, let's go."

He watched her lead the way through the living room and then turn and head up the stairs. He was still watching after he couldn't see her any longer.

"She's cool," Tony said. "The little boys need that."

He looked at Tony. "Anybody ever tell you that you're a wise kid for your age."

Tony hitched a shoulder. "I'm seventeen. I grew up fast, you know?"

"Yeah, I know." He looked at Greg. "Same goes for you. After everything you guys have been through, you could have given Mike and Gladys a hard time and had big chips on your shoulders like I did when I was your age. But you haven't. I'm proud of you." He stood. "Let's go upstairs and talk a few minutes." He led the way and they went upstairs and sank into the old recliners that were situated in the sitting area all the bedrooms opened up to.

It felt more comfortable here to him, given his feelings surrounding the changes below and all the money Caroline had spent without even asking him. Or needing him.

"I know y'all haven't seen them, because it's been

a busy day, I brought my colts over here I'm training."

"You did?" Greg's eyes flew wide with excitement. "You're training them?"

"Mike taught you, didn't he?" Tony sat up straighter, then leaned forward with his elbows on his jean clad knees.

Mike had been a quarter horse trainer in his early days and had trained several over the years that Jesse had been growing up on the ranch. But in the last ten years, Mike had stopped training and Jesse realized suddenly that the boys were missing an important part of his upbringing.

"Yeah, he taught me. He was really good at it. But he just did it part-time as a hobby after he and Gladys decided they wanted to turn the ranch in to a foster home."

"Could you teach us?" Greg asked, shooting Tony a look and getting a big grin from him.

"Yeah, we'd love to learn." Tony grinned.

He looked from one to the other, seeing keen interest. "Sure, I will. I'd love to. Tell you what, we'll start tomorrow after school. How does that sound?"

"Awesome," Greg jumped up and held his fist out for a fist bump.

He held his fist out and bumped Greg's then Tony's. "Okay, y'all head to bed. I'm glad to have y'all on board to help me with my horses."

The boys headed to bed a little bit later, talking excitedly about the new plan. He stood and started down the stairs when Caroline emerged from the younger boys' room.

"Hey," he said, pausing on the stairs to wait for her. She gave him a tired smile. "How did the story go?"

"It went well." She glanced at the area on the landing where he and Tony and Greg had been sitting. She took it all in. "This could be a great spot up here."

"It works. Me and the older guys had a good conversation up here, just relaxing."

"That's good." She smiled, seeming distracted as she moved past him and then started down the stairs.

Her soft scent tickled his nose and he followed her. "I guess we have a three-legged race to figure out," he said, struggling with something to say.

She stopped in the living room, looked around then reached over the back of the sectional and pulled a wrinkled throw blanket from the seat. He watched her fold it then place it at an angle on the new sectional couch.

"Yes, and a cake to bake or have baked. I'll look into it this week. We'll probably have to practice." She smiled. "The boys really loved the new furnishings. I was so glad. I was a little worried I might have made a few wrong choices, but they seemed really happy about everything. They're such great kids. I'm sorry you didn't like it but, in the end, this is about them."

He stared at her. She cared deeply for these guys. Unable to stop himself he gently pushed a strand of hair off her face, using it as an excuse to touch her soft skin. Her gaze searched his and he stepped toward her. Suddenly wanting more than anything to hold her, kiss her.

"You're great with them. You were amazing at the teacher meetings."

She held his gaze, her eyes searching his as she stood very still. He longed to cup her cheek, but sanity overrode stupidity and he let his hand drop back to his side as soon as he'd pushed the strand of hair behind her soft ear.

"Thanks…it was a great day. You never said whether you liked the new look." Her expression was hopeful.

"It's fine. The boys liked it." The words came out stiff, who was he kidding? He wanted her so badly and yet all of this reminded him of how little he had to offer her. "I need to go check on the horses."

She stared at him, her hopeful expression faltering as she pressed her lips into a flat line. She just stared at him for a heartbeat then looked away. "And I need to go to bed. Goodnight." There was an edge to her words.

He hated that he'd taken away her joy about what she'd done to the house.

He watched her walk through the kitchen and down the hallway toward their room. Frustration gnawed at him as he left the house through the front door and went to check on the horses. It was way past midnight, when he finally entered their bedroom, like the nights before, she was asleep, or pretending. He went to the closet and carefully pulled out his blanket and pillow and only when he went to stretch out on the couch did he realize it was new.

She'd thought of him when she'd decorated. The old lumpy too-short couch was gone. The new one was firm, more comfortable and fit his entire body from head to toe.

But it was still a couch and he was still six feet away from Caroline sleeping in that big bed alone. And despite all the reasons he knew he wasn't good enough for her, and all the reasons he knew he shouldn't want her. He did.

.

CHAPTER FIFTEEN

The next morning, Caroline woke before Jesse, rolled over and saw him sprawled on the new, wider, longer couch. He looked like he was sleeping well. Her gaze drifted over his relaxed features and down over his muscular shoulders and chest. She sighed…what was she doing?

Rolling over, she got out of bed and headed to the bathroom. No sense lingering and letting her mind go to wishes that would not come true. She had felt such a connection with him yesterday at the teacher's meetings, felt like they were a team. A good team working for the good of these five boys in their care.

She'd felt his withdrawal as soon as they'd entered the house and he'd realized how much she was changing it. He'd seemed okay when they'd first talked about it but she sensed that he was not as good with it as she'd first believed.

But that withdrawal hadn't stopped the fact that every time he looked at her…oh goodness gracious, her temperature had spiked. She felt like he wanted more from her than he was willing to let himself want. It came down to that darn money.

She climbed into the shower and let the hot water clear cobwebs from her brain. Her thoughts shifted to the boys. She'd been relieved and excited that the littles, the younger boys, had asked her to read to them. Her heart hurt just thinking about reading to them from the copy of Robinson Crusoe. She'd seen the book on the shelf earlier in the day and had immediately thought of the book. They'd loved her reading it so much that they'd asked her to continue reading it tonight. Her heart was full thinking about that.

How could she give all of this up?

She showered quickly and climbed out and was wrapping the yellow towel around her torso when she realized she'd forgotten to bring clothes into the bathroom with her.

She frowned at herself in the mirror. "How could you forget your clothes?" She grabbed another towel and rubbed her wet hair, the waves springing and tangling. Tossing the towel on the counter, she tugged her towel tighter as she cracked the door.

He was still sleeping. What was up with the guy this morning? He must have been exhausted too, neither one of them were sleeping well and that new couch must be comfortable.

She slid her gaze past him to the dresser where she'd stored her clothes. She bit her lip. Could she get over there and grab her underwear and her jeans and T-shirt. He was still sleeping, looked deeper asleep than before.

Sucking in a breath she clung to her towel and eased out into the room. She tiptoed slowly, her breathing was shaky and shallow as she eased past him. She was just five steps away from the dresser when her gaze strayed to him. He'd rolled to his side, his blanket had slid half off of him to the floor exposing his strong shirtless chest. *Why didn't he wear a shirt with his warmups? She didn't need to see all that magnificent skin.*

Yanking her attention back to the dresser she took another step, feeling a bit too much breeze beneath the towel for comfort.

"Well this is a surprise."

She whipped around at the sound of his voice. "What?"

He was leaning on an elbow, a lazy grin on his face. "If I'd known I'd be greeted by this sight in the mornings, I'd have slept late every morning."

She gripped her towel tighter and reminded herself she had on more than most people wore to the beach. "I don't always forget my underwear—I mean my clothes."

His brows rose. "I hope not, but it's made my morning interesting."

She glared at him, feeling far more aware of him than she wanted to feel. "Isn't it time for you to get up?"

He smiled lazily. "I'm fine right where I am."

"Ohhh, you," she huffed then marched, almost flounced but thought better of it, to the dresser. Didn't want the towel to bounce at the bottom too much. She carefully tried to pull the dresser drawer opened but with one hand holding the towel and only one hand to try and pull open the antique dresser's top drawer, it was awkward. Of course, it jammed. She gritted her teeth, then yanked, but that caused it to become slightly crooked. Now it wasn't going to open unless she used both hands and got it back on track.

Perfect. Just perfect.

She bit her lip and surveyed the things on the dresser but the lamp or the stack of thick books were not going to help her get this drawer pulled out. She heard a rustle behind her and slowly turned to find

Jesse sitting up, arms crossed as he watched her with a cocky grin on his handsome face.

"Looks like you're having a problem," he drawled, and despite herself, she shivered. "Maybe you should have replaced that dresser while you were shopping."

She narrowed her gaze. "Would you stop. Now come over here and open this for me. Or turn your head just in case while I yank on the drawer, I lose this towel."

He laughed. "If that's the case, maybe I don't want to help."

"I'm about to hurt you if you don't come over here." She laughed despite herself.

"Say please."

"I'm about to throw this thick copy of Gone with the Wind at you if you don't come help."

Grinning he stood. His warmups hung on his hips and his muscles flexed as he came her way. She realized having him so close to her might have been a very bad idea on her part.

"Okay, maybe I should go wait in the bathroom and you bring me my clothes."

He stopped next to her. His dark eyes searched hers. "Are you scared of me, Caroline?"

"No," she quipped. "Of course not."

"Then why won't you look at me?" his voice was low, gentle and made her light-headed when combined with his nearness.

She bit her bottom lip and then slowly lifted her gaze to him. Her stomach trembled and her knees followed. She heaved in a steadying breath as her mouth went as dry as West Texas in August. His dark eyes that were a deep grey shifted to black and he suddenly lost all cockiness.

"You sure are pretty first thing in the morning," his voice was raspy.

Ha, he was the pretty one in the morning, noon and night. "I think your eyes are blurry."

His lip hitched in a lazy, sexy grin. "My eyes are fine." He pushed a strand of damp hair off her face and she knew he was about to kiss her.

She breathed him in, lost sanity and leaned in…felt his breath feather across her lips and came to her senses. Stepped away from the gorgeous man she wanted a kiss from so much. But if she were to survive, she couldn't be kissing him.

She slipped away. "Just give that thing a yank and I'll grab my undies."

He looked disappointed then put on a smile. "Sure thing." He grabbed the handles and gave them a tug— and of course the drawer came right out.

She gripped her towel tight, reached past him and snatched a bra and panties and the first T-shirt off the stack beside her underwear. "Could you open the next drawer now, please."

His eyes twinkled at her. "As you wish." He pulled the drawer open and she stooped, grabbed a pair of jeans and then practically ran toward the bathroom.

Once inside she turned to close the door and saw Jesse watching her. There was a sad look on his face. Seeing her, he smiled and her heart squeezed tight with wishes she knew would never come true.

Stubborn man of her heart. Every day she was around him it was getting harder and harder not to let him see her true feelings. And that was just something she could not do.

* * *

"So how's it going between you two?" Ginny asked one day when she and Blaze had come over to help her paint the kitchen.

More trucks had been arriving all through the week and it had been a blitz of activity as she'd kept busy redoing everything.

"We're doing fine. You know, teamwork is the name of the game around here." She tried to sound optimistic. She was feeling stressed with every day that passed.

She caught Ginny and Blaze exchanging looks.

"What?" she asked, crossing her arms and letting her paintbrush dangle.

"You can talk to us," Blaze said.

"We've been in your shoes, remember," Ginny gave her a tell-it-to-me-straight look.

"Okay, I'm throwing myself into this house redo because I want to do what I can before my expiration date arrives. I'm completely frustrated with him. If I didn't have this project, I don't think I could make it the whole time. I'm not sure I can as it stands."

"I hear you," Blaze said, brushing the white paint on the cabinet door she was painting. "I think you love the guy and need to be straight with him."

She did not need to be talking about that. "Let's not go there."

"I think you need to," Ginny said. "It's clear you do."

"It doesn't matter. He doesn't want me. I knew that from the moment I agreed to this."

"Hiding your feelings isn't good for you," Ginny kept on. "You just need to get it out there in the open, clear the air and get it over with."

"Maybe we just need to paint. I need to go over

and see Allie and the baby. And talk to Nelda while I'm there. We have a school festival coming up and I need a cake. I'm hoping she'll bake one for me."

"Nice way to change the subject," Blaze laughed. "You know she will. That woman can bake a cake in her sleep."

"You should do that anyway, Allie might be able to talk some sense into you."

"I'm not going for advice, Ginny. I'm going for escape and relaxing."

"Whatever you say. I'll call Allie and tell her not to mention your sexy husband or the fact that you and him need to kiss and make up."

"Do not do that."

Ginny just grinned.

"So how much of the house are you painting," Blaze asked, having pity on her and changing the topic.

"I'm hoping to do all the rooms over the next couple of months before I leave. But painting is a huge undertaking I'll have to do it one room at a time. I don't want to displace the boys while I'm doing it."

"And it will keep her busy and give her a place to work out her love frustrations." Ginny waggled her brows.

Caroline laughed despite herself. "And yes, there is that too."

The day after they'd finished the kitchen makeover the boxes that she'd been waiting for arrived with great anticipation. She hadn't had time to go see Allie but she had called, and Nelda had graciously agreed to have a cake ready for her on Friday so she could take it to the festival on Saturday. That was one less thing for her to worry about.

The boys had loved every new thing she'd done with the house, the younger boys especially acted like it was Christmas every day after school. They'd come off the bus at a run and rush inside to see what new change she'd made to the house. Sometimes it was just decorations like pillows and rugs and pictures on the walls. Or a painted kitchen. It was so fun watching their reactions.

But today as she waited for them to arrive, she was especially eager. Earlier in the week she'd asked them to look through a website and pick out new covers for their beds. They'd been excited and the younger boys had asked every day since if their new covers had come in. Today as the boxes arrived, she'd barely contained her own excitement at the thought of how they would feel when they arrived home to find the changes.

She was just coming down from getting their beds made and had a few minutes to spare before they arrived on the bus. The door opened and Jesse walked in.

"Hey," she said, feeling that familiar surge of longing that had begun to be her constant companion. He looked tired, and she knew they were both running on fumes lately.

He'd been out somewhere on the ranch doing something with the cattle. She hadn't asked for specifics that morning, as they'd gone through their routine of getting the boys fed and on the bus. They'd brushed arms a few times as they'd passed each other, and that alone had set her insides to feeling jittery and the spring inside of her that seemed to tighten more and more each day coiled tighter.

"I was just about to get the boys a snack ready. Can I get you anything?"

He moved to the sink. "I can get it. What can I help you with?" He turned on the water then pumped some soap into his hands and began washing up.

"Oh, I've got it. But thanks." Feeling especially happy about the upstairs makeovers, she pulled open the refrigerator and pulled out the assortment of deli meat and the thick slab of cheddar cheese. The boys had really gotten into the cheese and deli snack. It was easy and wasn't a sugary snack, so she felt good about it too. Plus, it required no cooking. Sadly, she hadn't ventured out too much in that department still. And Jesse had seemed content to grill the meals in the evening and he seemed to love doing breakfast. Then, there was that niggling voice reminding her that she would be gone soon anyway, so why start cooking yet.

"That looks good." He turned, crossed his arms and watched her. "You look happy."

She paused slicing the cheese. "I am. I love when the boys come in from school. It's one of my favorite times."

His lip quirked and his dark eyes mellowed, mingling with her heartstrings in a connection she could not break. Oh, the man did something to her.

"They like it too."

She fought down the disappointment that he didn't say he liked it also. "Nelda is baking the cake for the festival. And I finished the signs first thing this morning."

"You did a great job on those. You worked hard enough on them."

"The boys helped. It was fun. They are excited about the festival and the three-legged race. Plus the cow chip toss." She laughed. "I still can't believe they are offering that. At least they are handing out latex gloves for it."

"I can't believe it makes you squeamish to think

about tossing a dried-up pile of cow poop." He laughed when she made a face at him.

"I might be a country girl but that part of country life I have never been into. I'll toss a frisbee with glee but not poop. That is a Texas tradition that some people loved, that and road-kill flattened armadillo shells. But those are two disgusting past-times I've never associated with."

He pretended shock. "I can't believe that."

She laughed. "You're like my brothers and my cousins, you loved it, I know. But then, y'all were once boys just like my boys."

The moment she said the words her heart skipped, and her gaze locked with his and she could tell that he had caught her "my boys" slip. Emotions rocked her and she looked back down at the cheese. They were her boys, it hadn't been a slip of the tongue but straight from her heart.

"Yeah, boys do tend to like things like that. It'll be a fun day." He hadn't called them his boys or their boys. He was instead skirting the issue. He was as aware as she was that their first month was quickly about to be finished. He had to also be aware that every day that passed was bringing with it new challenges and forever linking her heart here. Where he would get to remain. She was the only one being forced to leave. She wanted to shout out that it wasn't fair and yet she couldn't. She had signed on for this.

She had agreed. "Yes, they do. I'm just going to say, I didn't realize how attached I was going to get." Yanking up her big girl panties, she looked back at him and smiled. "You're a lucky man, Jesse James."

That all too familiar charge of electric raced through her as their gazes held. He started to say something just as the door was pushed open and Archie came bursting in red-faced and grinning. "I'm first!" He laughed as Kyle followed by Robbie came scrambling inside. They were all laughing.

"I thought I was going to beat you," Kyle said, falling against the wall holding his sides and breathing hard as he grinned.

"You can run too fast," Robbie yelled, grinning too. "My legs ain't long enough."

"That's okay, short stuff. I think you grew a centimeter this month." Archie settled into the barstool, grinning.

Caroline was smiling at them. "Y'all need to take your speedy selves over to the sink and wash up before you eat."

Robbie was closest to the sink and made a dive for it. He let out a whoop of glee when he beat the other two. She laughed and ventured another look at Jesse.

He met her gaze with an understanding expression. That gave her some satisfaction that at least he understood this wasn't easy for her.

Tony and Greg came sauntering in then, obviously not interested in joining in on the younger boys mad run from the bus drop off to the snacks.

"Hey, you two, wash up and then have a snack." She didn't want them heading up to their rooms just yet. They'd all do that after snack time.

"Sure thing," Tony said.

"Do we get to train today?" Greg asked Jesse.

"Yep, after you finish your homework."

Greg sighed. "We have a chemistry test tomorrow. It's going to be rough finishing studying up."

"Studies come first. But maybe you'll have a little time. We'll see."

They settled into snacking and Caroline could barely wait for them to finish. When they finally had eaten up everything she'd set out, she put her hands on her hips and smiled. "Now that you've finished, I'm thinking maybe you should all go upstairs to your rooms. Might be more pleasant studying up there tonight."

At her words, all eyes turned to her and then one of them gave a whoop and they all stampeded up the stairs. She looked at Jesse as he watched the boys disappearing up the stairs. She smiled, and then, not wanting to miss their excitement she followed them. She heard his boots behind her and knew he was coming too.

It was as wild as she'd anticipated. The entire house vibrated with their exclamations of excitement.

She reached the younger boys' room just as they all dove onto their new covers.

"This is so cool," Robbie said, laughing he rolled onto his back, his legs and arms wide.

Archie rolled to his side and propped his elbow up and leaned his head on the palm of his hand as he grinned. "Can we go to sleep now. I love it. Blue is my favorite color. And it feels like the skin on a baby rabbit."

He'd ordered a royal blue ultra-suede cover that was just as soft as he was saying it was.

Kyle scooted to the edge of the bed and kept his skinny legs dangling off the side as he set up and grinned. "This is the best. Did you order our new pillows too? I want to get the best sleep of my life." He laughed.

"I did and got new mattresses for you too."

They were all set up.

"Really?" Archie bounced up and down. "I thought it felt different."

They all then started chattering happily.

She left them enjoying themselves and went to Greg and Tony's room. Jesse had backed up to let her pass and hadn't said anything but a glance at him and she saw shadows in his eyes. Unease stirred and she wondered what he was thinking.

Greg sat on his bed looking about the room at the new dressers and curtains. "Thanks, Caroline. This is awesome."

"I'm glad you like it."

Tony hadn't sat on his bed. Instead he stood beside the bed, his hand touching the comforter. "It's really nice." He looked at her and the raw emotion in the laid-back teenager's face took her breath. "I've never had new covers and certainly never had anything I picked out myself," he said quietly.

Tears clogged Caroline's throat. "That doesn't mean you haven't deserved it, Tony."

He met her with eyes that she realized weren't sure whether to believe her or not. Her heart full in that moment. She looked at Jesse, it was a simple glance thinking he would understand the emotion that swept through her, but his expression was tight, unreadable.

"It looks good, Tony, and Caroline is right, you and all the boys deserve the best," he said. "Enjoy it, okay." And then he turned and headed down the stairs.

Tony sank to the bed and tested it out. He smiled. "I might get used to this. It feels good."

She smiled widely. "I thought so too." She held her smile but was very aware of the sound of Jesse's boots on the stairs. She heard him cross the living room and heard the door open then close. Emotions of confusion filled her as a few minutes later she left the boys all lounging on their new beds and made her way downstairs.

What was wrong with Jesse?

CHAPTER SIXTEEN

Caroline felt like she had a fist knotted inside her chest. The emotions the moments upstairs had filled her up with were tangled and messy and raw. She'd lost so much when she'd lost her mother and dad, but her grandparents had stepped in and worked so hard to ease loss with their love. She'd never lacked for anything money could buy or the security and love of her grandparents and her great uncle and aunt too.

She'd been hit full force with that while giving the boys new beds and bedspreads.

She'd wanted to give them the best of everything but it hadn't fully hit her how much she'd taken for granted in her own life.

And then Jesse had looked a little lost himself when he'd walked away and down the stairs. She realized now, he knew what these boys had been through. She didn't fully understand.

She found Jesse in the barn organizing bridles on hooks.

"Is something wrong?" she asked, her voice quiet not to bother the horses.

He spun, clearly having not planned on her following him. She waited in the doorway, feeling a coil tighten inside of her. It had been building ever since they'd started this dance on a tightwire they called a marriage.

He jiggled one of the bridles in his hand but said nothing, instead he continued what he'd started and hung it on a hook, before answering. "It's all so easy for you. If you want something, you just get it."

She sighed, emotion clawing at her. They were back to square one—the money. "Because I had the money to spruce up the house and give the boys new bedcovers for their rooms? Please tell me you're not wishing I hadn't done that?"

His gaze locked with hers and her answer was there, clearly written in his beautiful eyes.

Anger flashed hot and furious through her.

She'd had it.

Totally.

"Tell me you're not serious."

He rubbed his neck and looked at the ground. "No,

I wouldn't say that."

"Good. Because I can't read the signals you're giving off. And ever since I started sprucing the place up, that's what it feels like. That you might resent what I'm doing." She walked toward him, her heart pounding. "I'm trying to make the best of my time here. I'm trying to give these boys everything they need and deserve. I thought brightening up their rooms was a good thing. And yet you're out here sulking."

"I'm not sulking."

"Then are you mad that I did it? Because that's what I'm feeling. What do you want from me?" She stopped a couple of steps in front of him. The air between them seemed charged.

"I don't want anything. I was just frustrated." The last words were nearly a growl.

"By my money." It was totally clear. "I am so sick and tired of this. You look at me sometimes as if I were the best thing in the world and you actually care and want me. And before we got married, sometimes when we sparred verbally." She gave a gruff laugh remembering those moments that were, she knew ways they eased this frustration that came from wanting something that would never truly work. "At least I got some relief from these frustrations being around you fills me with. And it was fun in a crazy sort of way.

But now, even that's gone and…" She closed her eyes and sucked in a shuddering breath. "You act like you can just ignore this thing between us. This lie we keep telling ourselves that there isn't any real feelings between us. The lie we tell ourselves just because you can't handle the fact that I have money." The last part was said on a broken sob. There, it was out there. But she refused to cry. "News flash, Jesse James, I can't help who I am. And that you judge me for something I have no control over stings. I'm just trying to do good here." Her hands balled at her sides as feelings of so much helplessness that she'd locked away for so long boiled up and over. Again, she asked, "What do you want from me?" She wasn't going to make it here longer. Being here longer was just going to break her heart when she had to leave her boys. And him. And he didn't care.

He stared at her, his jaw clenched and unclenched, his gaze bore into hers…and then his arms were around her and he pulled her close and his lips crushed down on hers.

She was stunned at first and then she was kissing him, and he was kissing her. And like a fierce storm their emotions clashed with the force of a hurricane. As if he were trying to work out and expel a need inside of him.

She didn't care, she needed this. Wanted this.

All she cared about in that moment, just like that one time before when he'd kissed her, it felt so right. She didn't care if he were excorcising some horrible demon or not, all she cared was that he was finally kissing her again as it should be. As if they didn't have this money problem in between them. She kissed him with all of her heart and love, pretending they were on equal terms and she was the woman for him.

She clung to him, her fingers clutching his shirt as his fingers worked their way into her hair, and then moved to cup her face as his thumbs traced her cheeks caressed her skin as his lips shifted, sought to kiss deeper. Emotions filled her up and she clung to him. And he clung to her as their kiss drove the fear away and filled every wanting, lacking hole of her heart with love.

Love. With that single thought, sanity flooded back to her.

She wrenched her lips and body free of him. Stumbling back away from the shelter of his arms.

Breathing hard, she glared at him. "What am I thinking? I want to leave right now. But I'm not. I'm going to stick this out for the full three months and I'm going to walk away with my inheritance that bothers you so badly. I can do so much with it, more than just bedspreads and new couches. I can help change lives and just because you can't cope with it I'm not stopping what I'm doing and I'm not leaving."

"I didn't ask you to leave."

"But you know as well as I do that you would rather we didn't have to do this. You know how hard this is going to get in the next two months. And it doesn't have to be that way if only you could see me for who I am and not what I have." Her heart ached. Throbbed. She swiped the tears away, only then realizing she was crying. "I will do as I like for this ranch. I'll give the boys whatever I want because I can. It's things they need and deserve and it comes from my heart. Yes, just like you said, because I can and guess what? It isn't a dirty word. The sad thing is if you would just get over yourself and open your mind, and we worked together we could do so much good using my inheritance."

She backed away. "But never mind. This…won't ever happen again." She would not cry anymore. She was done crying.

Feeling empty, she turned and walked from the stables.

She was a fool. She'd been a fool for so long.

But no more.

* * *

Jesse watched Caroline storm from the stables, and he raked both hands through his hair, his hat having been knocked from his head during the kiss lay on the ground at his feet. He locked his fingers together at the base of his skull and stared at where she'd disappeared around the corner in the fading light.

Her words stung, dug deep and hit home.

She was right on target. He had the problem. It wasn't her. She couldn't help that she had the money. It wasn't her. And yet something in him wouldn't give. The money would always be a constant strife between them because he couldn't deal with it. Couldn't take it.

This had happened once before when he'd kissed her when they were in a heated exchange the year before they'd kissed again on their wedding day.

That first kiss had been like New Year's Eve in New York City. That time he'd been the one to tear away from the kiss that she'd so freely given into, so passionately embraced. She'd laid her heart out in that kiss and he'd backed off and told her it should never have happened. That her money would never let them have anything between them. He realized now that he'd been wrong. It wasn't her money, it was him.

Did he want her to be poor, have nothing and then she'd be good enough for him?

Wow. He was a number one jerk and yet what could he give her?

He spun and hung his elbows on the stall gate and lowered his head to the wooden gate. His head throbbed with the guilt and anger that warred inside of him. He should have never agreed to this wedding. He should have told Mike and Gladys he was the best man for this ranch and he refused to mess with Caroline's life in order to get the ranch. He should have told them that if they wanted him then it was with no strings attached. He should have done that.

He really should have. He lifted his head as the mare that had been standing in the corner of the stall staring at him with accusing eyes walked over and placed her jaw on his shoulder. He laid a hand on its mane and rubbed gently.

"I'm a fool. I know that's what you're thinking but Caroline needs someone who can give her what she needs, what she's used to." Even the words echoed hollow in the quiet stable. Could someone else give her the love she deserved and match her financially?

His gut tightened at the thought and he felt nauseous. He was a fool and yet he saw no way out. He was and would always be that kid who came from the bus station with nothing.

And she was the beautiful, spunky princess who deserved so much more.

CHAPTER SEVENTEEN

On Saturday they arrived at the festival site early. The boys were helping various groups set up, this had been organized by the teachers of the older guys and the middle school boys were also helping. That left Jesse and Caroline to set up their three-legged race together. Not that he could see there was a lot of setting up they had to do, but he had brought supplies to make the start and finish lines, some orange fluorescent paint was the most important part of the plan. That and the red ribbons Caroline brought to tie their legs together. They didn't really know what they were doing but they'd come prepared to figure it out. There were stakes and rope and prizes all stuffed in a box.

He carried the box as they walked out to the field where others were scattered around setting up. They hadn't talked a lot since the day in the barn. Caroline looked cute today, and his heart hurt every time he looked at her.

He had been noticing every little thing about her over her time at the ranch. How she paid such close attention to the boys, giving them all of her attention and her hugs each morning. It was easy to see they enjoyed the attention she gave them. And her smiles, those drove him crazy because he wanted more of them directed at him...after all, he was a boy too, at least at heart. Just watching her be the shaft of sunshine and joy that she was made his keeping his head straight harder and harder every day.

He thought about her constantly. He tried everything at night to get her off his mind. But it wasn't happening. Especially since the bathroom episode. And then their exchange in the stable two days ago. He could not get that moment out of his head.

Or his heart. He'd hurt her. And it was killing him but he couldn't fix this.

Mrs. Smith spotted them from where she was standing at a table loaded down with cakes. She smiled and hustled toward them. Caroline was carrying the cake that Nelda had baked for them. Without looking at him she then walked toward Mrs. Smith. He followed.

He figured at some point today she would have to talk to him. Yeah, he had messed up in a lot of ways but he wasn't exactly sure how to fix everything. He'd flirted a bit much while she was in that towel, and she'd been on edge ever since. He'd gone too far maybe in exposing the truth that was between them that he didn't want to acknowledge.

"Caroline, what a lovely cake. Did you make this, it's beautiful?" Caroline blushed. He didn't know that he'd ever seen Caroline McCoy blush but she looked pretty with her pink cheeks like that. *Okay, she could have had green spinach stuck in her teeth and he'd still think she was pretty.* He had it bad.

"I have to confess, Mrs. Smith. I'm a terrible cook and a worse baker. I can mix paint with the best of them but mixing ingredients is beyond me. Nelda baked it, you know she is the fabulous woman who works for my cousin, Wade, and his wife, Allie. She was so happy to be able to bake it and donate it to the cause. I want to give her the credit she's due and you are far better off that she did it than if I had baked it."

"I think that it's generous of you bringing this cake whoever made it. I know Nelda, lovely woman, please thank her for me. And thank you so much for enlisting her. Now I'll take this and you two can go out there in that field to your spot. I've marked it with a little sign on a stick. And I don't really know how far to mark off from the start line to finish line. I'll leave that up to you. Anything you need, just let me know. Did you happen to make any signs to let people know what your station is? Something bigger than my little sign?"

Jesse could have told the teacher that Caroline had worked really hard on the signs making them perfect with her artistic talent but he didn't. It would be evident when she put them up. Instead, he let Caroline do the talking.

"I did make signs, but I left them in the truck. We'll set everything up and then I'll go back and grab them so that the kids will know what in the world is going on where we're standing." She laughed. "Because I'm sure me and Jesse standing there with some strings in our hands is not going to send the message that there's anything fun happening at our station." She shot him a barely hidden glare.

Tension between them had been high since the kiss in the stable and her letting her emotions run free, and now those feelings were hitting their target again.

He held her gaze. "Yeah, we don't exactly say come on let's have a good time."

She hitched a brow. "You're right about that, Sheriff. Anyway, Mrs. Smith, please excuse us as we're going to go and see if we can't drag up a little fun. I'm sure that you and your Mr. Smith have a few days where life just doesn't seem fun anymore." Mrs. Smith bit back a smile. Her eyes were wide with a hint of alarm. Or laughter. He wasn't exactly sure.

"Caroline, you're right. We do have our days. But getting out and doing something different from your normal day to day activities helps, so you two run along and really have fun. Being out there at the ranch with a bunch of boys while you two are newlyweds has to be a bit stressful. Enjoy yourselves."

Jesse heard a note of censure in the last part. He gave her a sardonic expression he was sure though he tried not to. If she only knew what kind of pressure he and Caroline were feeling, she'd be shocked. "Yes, ma'am, we'll sure give it a go. How soon before the kids come over and, you know, mediate our little husband and wifely spat?"

The old woman did giggle then. "It will be about thirty minutes before we start, so please, you two, try not to kill each other before then. It's going to get better. Making up is always fun. And if you need more help come over here and buy a cake. Cake always helps."

Caroline gave the woman a I'm-not-so-sure-about-that look. "We might need a lot of cake," she said then with a short laugh started toward their area across the field.

He winked at Mrs. Smith before following Caroline. Her hair swayed in time with her hips and he decided it would have been better if he'd walked ahead of her. She was driving him crazier than he already was. This was going to be a long day.

When she reached the spot, she put hands on her hips and surveyed the area, then she turned and glared at him. "Alright, Mr. Happy. I guess we'll spray a line through here and then we'll go down there however far you think we need to be from the finish line and we'll spray a line there. Can you write Start and Finish with a can of paint?"

He gave her an exasperated stare. "I can do that. Are you going to do this all day?"

"Do what, Jesse?"

"You know what. Show me your temper? Look, I'm sorry."

The couple not too far from them who were setting up a bean bag toss looked their way and he realized they were talking too loud.

"Can we not talk about that here, please?" She'd realized they were drawing stares too. "We're supposed to look all happy and in love in public. Remember?"

"You weren't exactly looking happy in front of Mrs. Smith."

"She gets it, though. But the kids might see us looking all mad. You do have a look of a storm brewing on your face, Jesse James."

That had nothing to do with being mad. Frustrated, yeah, totally. "We've got to get past this."

"I'll get past it on my own timetable, thank you very much. Now, can we have a little less talking and a lot more action getting this setup done?"

"Yeah, sure thing, heiress. Anything you want." This was getting out of hand. And he wasn't sure how to handle it. He was in between a rock and a hard place. He wanted her but didn't know how he could ever have her. And he'd hurt her because of it.

"Caroline, we've got to get past this." She'd barely spoken to him since that kiss. Oh, when the boys were around she pretended well; he'd be surprised if they even realized there was anything wrong. He'd spent as much time out with the boys teaching them how to work with quarter horses and that had helped keep their interactions down. Which was good because like now, he wanted to pull her into his arms and tell her that he wanted her. That her money didn't matter, but it did.

She smiled at him. "I can fake it just as good as the next guy when the kids come around. Isn't that the agreement?" She turned and snatched the box out of his arms and then set it on the ground and started digging out the cans of spray paint, which she then slapped in his waiting hand.

"Ouch."

"Sorry."

"Yeah, right." Scowling, he started marking off thirty yards using his long strides to mark the distance. It gave him an excuse to burn off some steam and keeping himself from exploding there in the middle of the field where everyone would see him. When he reached approximately thirty yards, he turned, saw Caroline standing with her hands on her hips watching him.

Nope, that wasn't far enough distance between them and marked off another twenty yards. It didn't really ward off any more frustration, but at least it gave him an excuse to prepare himself for when he turned around and saw her glaring at him. She'd stuffed a fist to her slim hip that was jutted out and she had that sassy tilt to her head. And all he could think about was how bad he wanted to cross that distance and sweep her into his arms and kiss her right there in front of the whole town.

Nope, that was a bad idea. It was a really bad idea. There were people everywhere. Some boys were tossing a football nearby and other kids were scattered around as were teachers and parents getting ready. Not a good idea.

Instead he snatched the lid off of his spray can and started spraying a starting line parallel to where she stood at what would be the finish line.

Then he marched back to where she was now settling the ribbons on a small folding table and setting the awards out. She handed him the white can of spray paint. "Now do it again."

He'd do it again. He'd pull her in his arms and kiss her just like he had in the stables.

Bad idea but he wanted her and her pushing him now was not helping his situation.

He wanted to quiet her anger with a kiss. Yup, he had lost it. They hadn't lived together for more than a month. "How are we going to make it two more months like this?"

"I'm not sure," she said, quietly, just as a football slammed into her arm.

"Caroline," he said, dropping the can of paint to reach for her.

The boys with horrified looks on their faces reached them.

"We're sorry," the first boy said.

"Are you okay?" the other one asked as soon as he reached Caroline. "I didn't mean to hit you. It just slipped out of my hand."

She rubbed her shoulder. "It's okay, guys. I'm fine, really. Maybe go out away from the other people just a little further and have fun."

Jesse probably looked a bit sterner than Caroline. "Be a little more careful. Go on."

"Yes, sir," they said and raced off.

"I think you scared them."

"Are you okay?" He touched her arm.

"I'm fine. Really, I am. Now let's just get this done. We don't really have that much time and we can't do this in front of the boys."

He started to speak but she stopped him.

"I've got to go get the signs. If you'll mark this and then I think we'll be ready." With that she walked away. He watched her go, his gut twisted and for the first time in a very long time he wished that he was a wealthy man.

* * *

Caroline had to get a grip. Her heart pounded as she stormed away from Jesse. He had asked her how they were going to make it for three months. Good question.

She didn't think they could, but in the stables when she'd been so upset, she'd told him she would. They were going to have to find some kind of way to get past all this tension that they were feeling. If he had just not kissed her.

If he had just not crossed that line. She could have made it.

"No, you will make it," she muttered as she approached her BMW that was sitting beside Jesse's truck. Since they wouldn't all fit into his truck, she'd had to drive her car. She opened her passenger side door and reached for the posters that were rolled loosely and propped against the seat.

She would make it. She was walking away from this three-month ordeal with her inheritance, her dignity and her ability to spend her money on whatever she wanted too. Especially, to support her boys. Determination filled her up as she closed the car door and then headed back the way she'd come.

She saw Megan Benson, a teacher she knew, coming toward her.

"Caroline, wait up," she called.

She slowed. "Hey, Megan," She was glad to have a distraction from the thoughts churning in her head and heart. "It's good to see your smiling face."

"Yours too. Congratulations on getting married. I

always knew you and Jesse were in love." She smiled like so many others who had known she and Jesse would finally get married.

"Yes, you and a lot of others." Caroline gave a short, hopefully sincere sounding laugh.

"It's so exciting. And the boys just talk about you two all the time. They just love y'all. It's like y'all are a family now."

Caroline's world narrowed to the center of her heart where her love for them beat strong. "I'm crazy about them too." She wanted to say more but she couldn't. She would be gone in two months and what would Megan and others think of her then? But more importantly, what would her boys think of her?

"You and Jesse are in charge of the three-legged race, right?"

"Yes, we are."

Megan blushed. "Great. Last year all the teachers and adults had races also. It was fun and the kids enjoyed laughing at us. I was wondering if you planned on doing that? It would be fun, don't you think?"

Caroline hesitated, would that mean she would have to race with Jesse? "That sounds like it might be a fun idea." Not really. Maybe if she and Jesse weren't on bad terms...but this wasn't about just her and Jesse.

"Is there someone specific you're thinking this would be fun to do this with?"

The younger teacher's blush returned. "Well, actually, Coach Kramer just moved to town and I was thinking…that I could see if he wanted to race with me."

Caroline couldn't say no. "I'll see what I can do. Make sure you ask your coach."

"I certainly will. And I'll let the other teachers know too."

"Great." Caroline walked away wishing that her and Jesse's relationship could be simpler. But that had never been them, and never would be them. They were just a complicated mess.

By the time she got back to him, Jesse was waiting.

"I thought I'd lost you there for a minute. Thought maybe you'd loaded up in your car and left me here to deal with this on my own? I have to tell you I don't think I could handle it alone."

Her insides trembled as he looked at her with those deep, dark eyes. "I wouldn't do that. I committed to this and I'll see it through." It was true in all aspects of her life right now. "We better get these up."

He took the sign on a stake and while she taped one to the table, he took a hammer and gave the stake a few hits. "There, it looks good. I think we're ready."

The cowbell the principal was using to signal the start of each game sounded. It was time to begin. She and Jesse looked across the field at the podium where the high school principal stood with his megaphone in hand; he welcomed everyone. She shot a glance at Jesse. He was standing with his legs apart, his arms crossed, and he looked about as excited as a man about to go to the firing squad.

What was he thinking about so hard? Whatever it was, looking like that, he was about to scare a bunch of kids. "I guess we need to put on our happy faces, Sheriff."

He slid her a tense gaze, and she knew he was probably thinking about them and their problem. There was misery in his eyes for an instant, she forgot that they were in this love disaster because he couldn't see beyond her money.

She had to always remember that.

* * *

Standing beside Caroline, a storm of impending disaster was building inside of Jesse. It had grabbed him by the throat as he'd watched her walk away, heading to retrieve the signs. Watching her all he could think of was that soon, she would walk away and never come back. She would walk out of his life and his town, and he wouldn't get to see her dancing eyes challenging him when they'd see each other in town anymore. At least before this joke of a marriage, they had functioned on a level that enabled him to see her around town.

Now, she was going to leave and there were no guarantees she'd be coming back to town.

He wasn't sure he could handle that.

"Stop looking like you just buried your dog, Sheriff. You're going to scare the kids."

"Right." He shook off the feelings of dread. He didn't need to scare the kids. He forced a smile as the first kids raced up.

Caroline explained to the first group, how it would work and then sent him to the start line with them. He was glad to have the distance between them as he tried to get a grip.

When the younger kids up first were ready, he had to go down the line making sure they'd all tied their legs correctly. Then he stood back and held his arm up.

"On your mark. Get set. Go." He barely yelled the last word and the racers started their race of mayhem.

It was hilarious as the kids fell to the left and to the right, rolling all over the place with yelps and laughter. Some managed to do a great job but most didn't. He laughed watching until finally two sets of boys and a set of girls managed to get across the finish line. One of the sets of boys crawled over and fell to the ground laughing. Caroline was bent over she was laughing so hard as were the parents and teachers behind her. The two girls barely beat out the still standing set of boys who came in second to them. They were ecstatic and hugging each other and bouncing up and down and screaming in delight. You'd have thought they'd won the Publishers Clearing House Giveaway or something.

The set of boys laying on the ground had started a trend and as the others made it across the finish line those that were still standing and not crawling fell on the ground laughing.

It was a pileup like nothing Jesse had ever witnessed. This was a pretty fun game. Next the teenagers lined up and it was really wild. It didn't last long and was just as fun as the little kids. During all of it his gaze kept roving to Caroline. She was, as usual, a ray of sunshine and was having a blast.

The regret and discontent that had been building in him strengthened. And amid all the laughter his smile faded as the thought of her walking away for good took over like a fever and saddened him to his very core.

CHAPTER EIGHTEEN

Caroline hadn't had so much fun in a very long time. And she was thankful for it because it distracted her from thinking about Jesse and the mess they were in. Her gaze had strayed to him a few times and he looked as if he were enjoying the races too, laughing and looking more gorgeous than should be right for a man. She was laughing hard at Greg and Tony who had believed themselves invincible and were now crawling over the finish line like so many other teams. Poor Robbie and his buddy Drew had had to do the same thing earlier. Kyle and Archie had been the only of her five boys to make it across standing and they were now lording it over the older boys.

She was laughing at their antics when her gaze found Jesse again. He had his shoulders back and was watching her and he wasn't laughing. Her heart cinched tight because even at this distance he looked alone and sad down there at the starting line by himself.

She yanked her gaze away from him, unable to handle the distraction right now. She glanced over and saw the group of teachers and parents that had gathered on the sidelines and a smiling Megan grinned as she pointed to the handsome man standing beside her. That was obviously Megan's coach.

She saw Jesse striding her way, probably thinking the races were over. She waved her arms. "Alright all you winners gather up over there. But before we hand out the medals, we have one last race. Who wants to see the adults race?"

A cheer went up from the kids and so she called for the teachers and parents to come forward.

Tony, wearing a huge grin came over. "You and Jesse have to do it too. Me and Greg can man the start and finish lines. I'll set them to go and Greg can stand here to watch who comes over the finish line and wins."

"That's okay—"

He made a face. "No, we want to see y'all do it too."

Robbie and the other boys came over and joined in. Jesse had reached them, and they started pressing him about them racing. His gaze connected to hers and she could see he was not on board either. She wanted so much to just say no. No way. But she couldn't deny the boys' excitement.

"I guess you and me are racing. Are you ready?"

He did not look ready but he put on his game face for the guys. "We've got to do better than those two." He winked at Greg and Tony, who just rolled their eyes and laughed.

She hit Jesse's arm as they walked toward the start line. "You go easy on them. It was obvious the girls had practiced, and the boys hadn't."

"People practice for this?"

She laughed. "If they want to win, they do."

"Well if that's what it takes, then I think me and you might as well give it up now."

"Hey, don't give up before we start. I'm pretty competitive and you know I want to beat these people. I never give up without a fight."

"True. Then I guess you and me need to call a truce right now."

"I don't know about that, but with your long legs and my long legs, I'm guessing we should be able to do a pretty good job if we just work together."

He looked at her as they reached the starting line. "I'm beginning to wonder if we can do that."

She let his words slide off of her, wondering the same thing and she knew neither one of them were talking about the three-legged race. She set her jaw. "Tie this around our connecting legs. Not too tight, you know we need to have a little room to move."

As he bent to tie the ribbon, she ignored the thumping of her heart and the electrical zingers ricocheting through her as his leg and her leg made contact. For a distraction from his touch tying the ribbon, she looked around and saw the laughing adults all looking about as excited to do this as the kids. Megan and her coach looked adorable. She figured there probably was a good chance that those two would be married in the next year or so. They definitely had chemistry going on. Then again, she looked at Jesse's dark head as he finished tying their ribbon, there was chemistry between them and that didn't mean anything where they were concerned.

He stood. "Alright, we're ready."

She swallowed hard, looking at him. They had to wrap their arms around each other now. "We wrap our arms around our waists," she said though it was unnecessary.

She hadn't even thought about having to hold onto him. He looked about as hesitant as she was.

Greg hollered, "On your mark."

Jesse gritted his teeth, his jaw locked as he slid his arm around her waist.

"Get set."

She locked her arm around his hips, all too aware they were plastered together now. He looked down at her and she looked at him. For a moment that heat from two nights ago with the kiss shadowed his eyes, she looked away.

"Go." Greg finished making the call and instantly everybody went into motion.

She and Jesse started forward with their tied legs first. His stride was longer than hers just a little but it was enough to get them off-balanced, they stumbled but managed to stay standing. Some of the people all around them were falling and some were making a move ahead of them, but he had locked his jaw and he was gripping her waist hard as he tried to get them a few more feet down the grassy pasture. Someone fell beside them and she glanced over and saw that it was Megan and her coach. They were giggling and rolling around and Caroline got distracted by how happy they looked. When the coach rolled over and ended up with Megan on top of him grinning mischievously, Caroline got so distracted that she missed her footing.

In the next instant she was off-balanced and she fell, and Jesse came down with her.

They rolled and he was trying to take the brunt of the hit by spinning and yanking her on top of him when they landed. He grunted as she landed on his chest looking down at him. Then they rolled and he ended up with her beneath him. She was panting, breathing so hard as laughter bubbled out of her. He lifted on one elbow and looked down at her with serious, searching eyes.

She chuckled again, unable to help it, better to laugh than cry. She wanted him in her life for good so badly she couldn't stand it.

And then he laughed. "Are you okay?"

She could hardly breathe, her laughter busting out of her died in her throat. She was so aware of him. His gaze fell on her lips and all she could think about was kissing him. She was doomed. Doomed.

So doomed…panic rocked her. "I need…to get up," she was breathless, gazing into his searching eyes as longing nearly overwhelmed her. She scrambled out from under him. But they were still tied together. She fumbled, found the ribbon and yanked. He'd tied it with a calf roping knot and it fell away in an instant and she was free.

Like a woman running from a stalker, she scrambled up and hurried toward the finish line.

* * *

Jesse sat up and his mood darkened as he watched Caroline fleeing his presence. He'd wanted more than anything to kiss her moments ago. And he almost had. If she hadn't scrambled from beneath him, he might have done it. And then what? Everyone in town would see them kissing?

He made it sound like such a horrible thing, when it wasn't—they were, after all, married. But it was because if he kissed her again it would be one too many times he'd have crossed that line on what was acceptable in this fake marriage they had going on.

He stood up, and followed her to the finish line where she was now handing out the awards. His heart was hammering so hard he thought it would beat a hole through his ribs.

"Are you going to give in to your feelings for my sister?"

The man's voice had him turning to find Ash standing beside him. "Where did you come from?"

"Me and Holly brought Tess. You know she started kindergarten. We thought she would enjoy the games. We just got here a little late. But not too late to see the fireworks flying off of you and Caroline just now."

"It wasn't what you think."

Ash gave him a I'm-no-fool look. "You want to tell that lie to someone else because I'm not buying it. When are you going to wake up and take hold of what everyone else knows is true? You and Caroline are meant for each other."

Not wanting anyone else to hear the conversation he started walking away and like he assumed he would, Ash came with him.

"We're just doing this to save the ranch and her inheritance. That's it."

"Maybe that's why you two decided to do it. But I can't help thinking you both did it because deep down you care."

He stopped walking. They were back at the starting line and no one was around. "Ash, come on, what do I really have to offer your sister? Nothing. I have nothing to offer her. And don't say I have love. Because even if I do, that is not enough. A man has to be able to—"

"To what?" Ash scoffed, very unlike him. "Have more money than her in order to love her?"

"Well, yeah, in order to be viable to the relationship."

Ash didn't hold any punches with his disdain. The boyish-looking veterinarian had steel in his voice.

"Listen carefully to those words. And think about the box you're putting my sister in. I've always figured it was going to take a man with a lot of self-confidence to be able to handle loving Caroline. I've always thought that was you. Granddaddy obviously does too."

The irony of the words rotted on his stomach. People on the outside looking in didn't see the boy he'd been. The kid who'd come from nothing. "I'm not good enough for her."

Ash looked at him in disbelief. "Is that so. I'm not sure what man you're thinking about when you say that. But we are obviously not looking at the same man in the mirror when it comes to you."

* * *

Caroline couldn't sleep. They'd arrived home from the festival and the kids had been so excited. She and Jesse had spent the evening avoiding each other. She'd gone up and read to the boys and when she'd come downstairs, she'd known he wouldn't be in the house. She knew he was out in the stables, giving her time to go to bed. Feeling keyed up and fed up she took a deep breath to steady her nerves. Then she opened the back door and walked out onto the porch. She'd gone over and over this in her mind and she knew that this was the only way. She knew what she wanted. And she'd thought about him ever since they'd fallen on the ground tangled up with each other.

She wanted to be tangled up with Jesse James for the rest of her life. And it had hit her as she'd been sulking and feeling sorry for herself that in any other part of her life she would go after something she wanted. She was pretty fearless until it came to Jesse.

Why was that? Because she knew he didn't want her or that her money intimidated him...and she felt weird confronting him about that. In the barn the other night, she'd confronted him but she hadn't stated her case. Hadn't told him she wanted him forever in her life.

To her surprise, he wasn't in the stable. She looked around and petted one of the horses that came and greeted her. She decided to walk around the back of the stable and she found him sitting on a tractor blade they used to rake the dirt in the arena to keep it soft for training the horses.

There was a full moon tonight and he was clearly outlined in the light of the moon. The crunch of her shoes on the gravel drew him to look in her direction.

"Caroline. What are you doing?"

"I've come to talk."

"Yeah, we should." He stood and she felt the overwhelming need to run to him and wrap her arms around him.

"Jesse, I'm just going to tell you that I love you. I've loved you for so long…and I know you can't get past my money."

"Caroline, wait." He crossed the space between them and placed his hands on her shoulders. But she was not planning on waiting.

"I came here to lay my heart out bare to you. I want you. I want these boys. I feel like they're mine and I don't want to give them up. I wanted to be angry. I wanted to be strong and to walk away, but I can't."

"I have nothing to give you. Don't you know I love you too, that I want you. It hurts my heart knowing I can't have you, but I can't face not ever being able to give you things you need and want. You don't or won't ever need me."

Tears sprang to her eyes. "Oh, but you are so wrong. Jesse, you can give me the most important things my money can never buy. Your love and my boys. And this ranch and a life here with all of you is what I want. Jesse, as you can see, all the money in the world can't buy me that. Only you. Only you have the power to give that to me. But to do that you have to put down your pride, just like I'm doing right now. I'm putting down my pride, laying my heart and soul bare to you and giving you the power to reject me." She'd never felt this vulnerable before, except when she'd learned her parents had perished. "I'm just letting you know how I feel. And you have the next several weeks to decide. I just wanted to be honest and open."

They stared at each other and in the distance the coyotes cried to the moon.

She held back the scalding tears that were threatening to let loose when he said nothing. She turned and walked away.

Her heart hurt so much at his silence. What had she expected? That he would go down on one knee and asked her to marry him? Ha, they were already married and what a joke that was. No, she'd bared her soul and now it was all up to him now.

* * *

Jesse watched the woman he loved walking away. That sense of impending doom that he'd been feeling today crashed down around him. He knew what it had cost his proud, sassy Caroline to bare her soul like she'd done. She'd opened her heart and given him the power to devastate her. Break her heart and send her away.

Say something.

Don't let her go.

You're losing her.

He stepped forward. Everything in him screamed for her. All he had to do was lay down his pride. Just like she'd done.

Jesse, you can give me the most important things my money can never buy. Your love and my boys.

Her words echoed in his head and demanded his full attention.

Ash had said basically the same thing today.

All the money in the world can't buy me that. Only you. Only you have the power to give that to me.

She disappeared around the corner of the building...time ticked away in his head. He saw everything he'd ever really wanted within his grasp. He just had to go after her.

In that moment he broke out into a run.

His heart pounding out of his chest he rounded the corner of the building and skidded to a halt. She was halfway between the stable and the house.

"I want you, Caroline. Only you and our boys. And I'll do whatever it takes to keep you."

She turned and in the moon's light he saw her wet

face. He burned up the space between them and took her beautiful, dear face between his hands. "I love you." She gasped at his words and he continued, "And I've been a fool. There is no way I can ever let you walk out of my life. You are my life. You and the boys and what we can build here. You and me together. The boys would be as devastated if you left them. And I would be too. If you want me, I'm blessed by it and I'm all yours. Always."

She nodded and when her arms went around his waist, his lips lowered to hers.

He drank her in, unable to believe she was giving him this gift. So thankful that he hadn't let his pride cause him to lose her.

When he broke the kiss, he rested his forehead against hers. "You've made me the happiest man alive. I sure hope you know what you're getting yourself into."

She breathed him in and laid her head on his shoulder as she clung to him. "I do. Jesse James, we're going to build a life here on this ranch where we make a difference in the lives of our boys we have now and our boys we will have. You and I are a team and together, we're going to be unstoppable."

He chuckled and everything fell into place.

"Caroline James, I love the way you think."

She looked up at him and grinned with that mischievous glint in her eyes. "Good, then carry me across that threshold and let's get this real marriage started."

Laughter bubbled from him. "Yes, ma'am, I do like the way you think." And then he lifted her into his arms and strode toward the house. He couldn't get there fast enough.

EPILOGUE

With Penny acting as the host they threw a huge wedding reception at the ranch the following month. Caroline's heart was full of love as she watched all of her friends and family gathered to celebrate her and Jesse's marriage.

Her boys all looked so handsome in their new boots and western attire. Her heart was so full as she watched them enjoying the music and even dancing a bit. She and Jesse had already danced their wedding dance, and he was in conversation with her brothers a few feet away from her. And she was taking a moment just to enjoy the view. Her world was complete.

"Caroline."

She turned to find her granddaddy. He was the one aspect of this that she hadn't yet faced. He still didn't know that she and Jesse had become a real couple. She still held a bit of a grudge for the way things had been done.

"Granddaddy."

He crooked his arm. "Walk with me?"

"Okay, we need to talk." She slipped her arm in his and they walked away from the crowd toward the stables.

"How are you?"

"I'm good. How are you?"

He gave her a sad smile. "Missing you. I know my heart has been in the right place, but with you, I was never sure I handled it right. Darlin', I don't want to lose you."

Her heart ached and swelled with love for this man. "You aren't. You're right, you were brutal. But I get why you did it. And I thank you for it."

He stopped walking. "You thank me for it?"

She looked at him and nodded as a smile swept across her face. "You were dealing with two prideful, stubborn individuals who needed help. We needed tough love and I'm thankful for your crazy intervention."

"Are you telling me that you and Jesse are happy now?"

She smiled. "Yes. We worked out our…problems two weeks ago. I love him so much, Granddaddy. And if we hadn't married to save this place and the boys we both love, I don't think we would have ever been brave enough to face our love for each other. Thank you for sticking to your guns and forcing us to come together for a greater cause. I'm so grateful to you."

She leaned in and kissed his cheek and he hugged her tightly.

"It was one of the hardest things I've ever done, Caroline. I'm so happy for you and Jesse. You two are going to be a powerhouse and I can't wait to see all you do together."

"Me either. We've got ideas but for now, we're focusing on the boys we have now. And adjusting to our new life truly together."

"I think that's a good place to start and you know I'm always on your side for anything you need me to help with."

"Yes, I do. And believe me, I'm going to call on you a lot. But right now, I'm going to go dance with my husband."

They started back toward the group. Jesse saw her coming and when they reached him, she walked into his arms. "He knows," she told him and he smiled.

"Talbert, I owe you for your off the wall meddling. I'm in love with your granddaughter and thank you for giving me the time to realize I couldn't let her go."

"You're a good man, Jesse. Now dance with your wife. This is y'all's celebration, after all."

Jesse took her hand. "That's the best idea I've heard all night."

And then he led her onto the dance floor, took her in his arms and held her close. "Dance with me for the rest of my life?"

She leaned her head back and met his dark gaze. "You just try and get rid of me. You're stuck with me now, cowboy."

"Like glue, heiress. Like glue."

She laughed as they two-stepped onto the floor. "Perfect. That's music to my ears."

And it was. Sweet, sweet music.

Don't miss the next book in this series,
HER BILLIONAIRE COWBOY'S
INCONVENIENT MARRIAGE BLESSING.

About the Author

Hope Moore is the pen name of an award-winning author who lives deep in the heart of Texas surrounded by Christian cowboys who give her inspiration for all of her inspirational sweet romances. She loves writing clean & wholesome, swoon worthy romances for all of her fans to enjoy and share with everyone. Her heartwarming, feel good romances are full of humor and heart, and gorgeous cowboys and heroes to love. And the spunky women they fall in love with and live happily-ever-after.

When she isn't writing, she's trying very hard not to cook, since she could live on peanut butter sandwiches, shredded wheat, coffee...and cheesecake why should she cook? She loves writing though and creating new stories is her passion. Though she does love shoes, she's admitted she has an addiction and tries really hard to stay out of shoe stores. She, however, is not addicted to social media and chooses to write instead of surf FB - but she LOVES her readers so she's working on a free novella just for you and if you sign up for her newsletter she will send it to you as soon as its ready! You'll also receive snippets of her adventures, along with special deals, sneak peaks of soon-to-be released books and of course any sales she might be having.

She promises she will not spam you, she hates to be spammed also, so she wouldn't dare do that to people she's crazy about (that means YOU). You can unsubscribe at any time.

Sign up for my newsletter:
www.subscribepage.com/hopemooresignup

I can't wait to hear from you.

Hope Moore~
Always hoping for more love, laughter and reading for you every day of your life!